"I am glad we are all together again."

The *contessa* smiled and concluded firmly, "Now things can be different. Perhaps I shall live to see you settled at Cerano and happily married, Tarquin."

So Tarquin and Emmy were not yet married! A mad, wild delight flooded into Harriet's heart only to be immediately quenched by the look in Tarquin's eyes.

"I have no thought of marrying at present," he said coldly. "Other things must come first."

"Don't wait too long," advised the *contessa*. "The years pass quickly, and there is no substitute for happiness."

Harriet recalled the wedding almonds the young, unknown bride had given her to wish her well. But her heart froze as she remembered how her own happiness with Tarquin had been destroyed one year ago!

OTHER
Harlequin Romances
by JEAN S. MacLEOD

Many of these titles are available at your local bookseller.

For a free catalogue listing all available Harlequin Romances, send your name and address to:

HARLEQUIN READER SERVICE,
M.P.O. Box 707, Niagara Falls, N.Y. 14302
Canadian address: Stratford, Ontario, Canada N5A 6W2

Brief Enchantment

by

JEAN S. MacLEOD

Harlequin Books

TORONTO · LONDON · LOS ANGELES · AMSTERDAM
SYDNEY · HAMBURG · PARIS · STOCKHOLM · ATHENS · TOKYO

Original hardcover edition published in 1979
by Mills & Boon Limited

ISBN 0-373-02366-9

Harlequin edition published November 1980

CHAPTER ONE

IT was good to come back to Rome in spite of the fact that her heart had been torn asunder when she had once lived there. Harriet Voyle, librarian, looked out of the plane window at the rolling countryside of Latium bounded by the volcanic Alban hills. She saw the Tiber shining in the sun and Hadrian's Tivoli on its ancient hill, and all of Rome glittering beneath her, and suddenly her breath caught in her throat and the old doubt asserted itself as she wondered if she should have come at all. It was almost three years since she had first come to the Eternal City to work for the Contessa Renata de Filippo and a year since she had gone back to London in near despair, putting two years of her life firmly behind her and most of her loving.

Why, then, had she decided to return? Because the Contessa had been more to her than a mere employer; because Renata de Filippo had offered her a friendship lost to her by the death of her own mother in London six months ago. Yet the Contessa's friendship had failed to keep her in Rome after the tragedy of Carlo Luciano's death and her own unhappy involvement.

She gazed down at the glittering, sprawling metropolis on its seven hills with the roads that led to it fanning out in all directions—to the sea; to the mountains; to the north; to the south, the famous highways which still bore their ancient names to conjure up the grandeur of the past when Rome was still the gladiator city which ruled the western world.

The plane banked and turned, like a silver bird in the early-morning light. They were about to land. Harriet drew in a deep breath, her hands fastening on the soft travelling bag which she had bought on the Via Condotti in a burst of enthusiasm for the finest leather she had ever seen. She would be met, of course. Graziana would be waiting at the airport and they would talk about everything and everybody except Tarquin.

She thrust the past away, unable to deal with it and the near-excitement of the present. If her heart was beating with a wild expectation it would soon be crushed as Graziana recounted the events of the past missing year in her clear American voice. Much water had flowed under the bridges of the Tiber since she had walked with Graziana through the ancient streets of Rome. They were older and less carefree now; they had both been hurt by love.

The airport at Fuimicino was crowded even at such an early hour, but she made her way with the knowledge of experience to where Graziana would be waiting. They would have difficulty in getting a taxi, as it was obviously a holiday and the Romans were on the move. The whole waiting area was full of them, immaculate, aloof-looking men and elegant women; families in garrulous little groups; old couples anxiously guarding their luggage, all listening for the intimation which would take them to a modern magic carpet ready to fly them towards their hearts' desire.

Harriet searched among them for Graziana's familiar smile. Of course she would come. Had they not made a pact that, should Harriet ever return to Rome, Graziana would be there to meet her? She would be there, however far she had to travel, and Graziana Carducci kept her promises.

'Hi! So you really are here at last!'

They were in each other's arms, Graziana's warm cheek pressed against her own, her full bosom heaving from the effort she had made to reach the airport on time.

'You're all out of breath,' Harriet said, holding the younger girl at arms' length to look into the bright, dark eyes she remembered so well. 'What happened?'

'Nothing out of the ordinary. You know what Roman traffic is like!' Graziana's light American accent belied her utterly Italian looks. 'You've no idea how glad I am to see you again. It's been far too long.'

They stood in a little awkward silence, remembering the past, until Graziana said too quickly:

'If we stay here we'll be swept away. Have you much luggage?'

'Just what you see, so we can get the airport bus. It'll be cheaper than a taxi and maybe quicker,' Harriet decided.

Graziana hesitated, a deep colour staining her cheeks, and for the first time Harriet became aware of a new reserve in her.

'We're being picked up,' she said with the reluctance which generally covers acute embarrassment. 'Grandmother insisted on it.'

Harriet drew in a deep breath. There could be only one reason for Graziana's hesitation, for her reluctance to inflict hurt by mentioning Tarquin's name.

'We could have managed on our own,' she said stiffly. 'There was no need to bring Tarquin to the airport to meet me.'

'I didn't bring him,' Graziana objected, looking beyond her. 'But he must have been willing to come since he's here.'

It was almost more than Harriet could do to turn and look at Tarquin in that first moment of shocked surprise. She had known all along that she would probably meet him again, married to Emmy Luciano, but hope and a desperate, stubborn love had pushed the realisation of this new despair to the back of her mind. There had been no word of him for months, no mention of his beloved name even in the letters which the Contessa had written, asking her to return, but he must have been sure of his new-found happiness when he had agreed to meet her like this. The coldness of death was in her heart as she turned to greet him, knowing that she would find him changed.

He strode towards them between the waiting Romans, taller than most of them, a dark, introspective man in a grey suit and fine silk shirt with his hat in his hand but no welcoming smile in his eyes. In that moment words seemed to be impossible between them. Harriet sought for a conventional greeting and failed to find one, while Tarquin's almost disinterested gaze turned her heart to ice. Once he had held her in his arms, kissing her hair with a tenderness she had misunderstood; once she had imagined that he loved her, but that was long ago, a world away. He had been young then, the spirited gladiator with the future to conquer, and she had been his willing slave. So much for the thoughtlessness of youth! They had laughed and played together, swimming in the green water among the rocks at Amalfi, and the sun had shone each day out of a clear blue sky so that nothing had seemed impossible, not even the fact that she might one day marry the Contessa's grandson and live happily ever after.

'I'm glad you've come,' he said briefly. 'My grandmother needs you.'

That was all. Her return to Rome had only to do with the Contessa and herself. The brevity of his greeting and the words in which it was couched made everything quite clear. The days she remembered in the Amalfi sunshine were not even a memory to him. They were hers alone, her own pitiful little imaginings, the trembling joys to which she had clung so stubbornly for a whole long year. Tarquin had fashioned his life in another way and the dark, closed face he presented to her now was that of a stranger.

'How is the Contessa?' Her voice sounded hollow in her own ears, reflecting all the torture of her sudden pain. 'She wrote to me from Capri, but I expect she has now returned to Rome.'

He shook his head.

'She is still at the villa. She wishes you to go there.'

'I was about to tell you,' said Graziana, looking from one of them to the other with a strange expression in her dark eyes. 'She hasn't been well, so she's stayed at the villa all winter. Rome doesn't really suit her, although she loves it dearly.'

The thought of Renata de Filippo's illness banished some of the pain from Harriet's heart.

'She didn't mention being ill,' she said as Tarquin made a way for them through the crowd. 'What happened?'

'She says she's become old and weak, but that's just poppycock!' The Americanism fell glibly from Graziana's full, red lips. 'Can you imagine my grandmother not being able to cope with life, even if old age is creeping up on her? But she's decided to stay at Anacapri until you get there. Then, I understand, she will make other arrangements.'

Harriet followed at Tarquin's heels, aware of his every movement, of the dark, shapely head held unconsciously high and his clear grey, English eyes gazing straight ahead as if he saw only one destination in the whole world which did not include her. Aware of the old magnetism which was in no way diminished for her, she fixed her gaze on his uncompromising back view as they came at last into the full light of the morning sun, knowing that it exuded the same strength and determination of purpose which had first attracted her to this man, although there was no suggestion of kindness in him when he turned to look at her.

'I am to take you to Anacapri,' he said. 'Today is a holiday in Rome, as you may remember, and we have the whole week-end at our disposal.'

Harriet drew nearer to Graziana.

'I should have remembered about the holiday,' she acknowledged. 'I thought we would be going straight to the shop.'

'The shop is closed for the moment,' Graziana explained, gazing at Tarquin's unresponsive back. 'That's part of the reason why you've been sent for. My grandmother can no longer manage it on her own.'

It had never occurred to Harriet that she had been asked to return for any other reason than to help the Contessa with her very lucrative business as a dealer in silver and old and valuable books. She had been employed at the shop in Rome for over a year and had travelled to and from London on behalf of the Contessa in search of the old volumes in which she specialised, but it was only towards the end of her sojourn in the city that she had come to know the family. The Contessa was a kind employer, but she was also a proud Roman whose inner family circle was a jealously-guarded citadel to which strangers were rarely admitted until they had proved their worth. Harriet had met Tarquin at Amalfi, where the Contessa had taken a holiday villa, but even although she had proved a dependable assistant she had never been invited to the Villa Ilena on the family estate.

Amalfi had proved wonderful enough, and they had all been very happy there.

It seemed a hundred years ago, she thought, following Tarquin out of the shadows into the bright light of the Italian morning.

'We will have something to eat before we start,' he suggested. 'It is still very early.'

'I had breakfast on the plane. It was really quite adequate.' Harriet turned to wait for Graziana. 'Of course, you are coming with us?' she said.

Graziana shook her head.

'I wish I could,' she said, 'but there's so much to do. Soon I'll have exams to sit and I'm expected to pass them.' She made a wry little face which belied the sparkle in her dark eyes. 'If you can tell me what arithmetic has to do with art, I'll be obliged. I never could count, and decimals mean nothing to me at all.' She sighed. 'Who was it who said that the Fates demand untold sacrifices for our desires?'

'Nobody, I expect,' said Tarquin, taking her by the elbow. 'I hear you have acquired a car.'

'*And* a driving licence!' Graziana told him. 'I meant to take Harri for a spin this afternoon to San Felice, I thought.'

'She will be safer with me,' her cousin predicted. 'What sort of car have you managed to acquire, may I ask?'

'It's a Bugatti—a very old one,' Graziana admitted, 'but it's still quite fast.'

He frowned.

'You'd be safer on the bus.'

'Not much, and it wastes so much time having to queue

in the rush hour,' Graziana pointed out. 'Besides, I'm always burdened with a sketching-block or something when I have to hold on for dear life at a corner! No, a car is the only answer, as you're well aware, even if it is only a ten-year-old model with an open top.' She halted at the curb where a sleek grey Mercedes-Benz was parked. 'You won't want to know me when you see the Bugatti,' she declared.

Tarquin stooped to open the door of the Mercedes, the hint of a smile hovering in his eyes.

'I'm prepared for anything,' he declared. 'Where are you parked?'

'Miles away,' Graziana told him lightly. 'I'm hardly in the VIP class! Don't wait for me, since I can't come with you,' she added briefly. 'I'll see you next week when you come back to Rome. See you, too, Harri,' she added. 'Have a nice week-end!'

She had gone before they could detain her, a modern American girl who had felt the pull of her parents' homeland and come to Rome to study under her Italian grandmother's wing. She had been two years in the metropolis without achieving very much, but now it seemed that she was a little more serious about her ambitions, a fact which the old Contessa was sure to applaud. Although he had no real responsibility where Graziana was concerned, Harriet knew that Tarquin was prepared to keep an eagle eye on his young cousin. Eight years her senior, he knew all the pitfalls she was likely to encounter in the Eternal City and the very fact that she considered herself a sophisticated product of the New World was certainly one of them. At eighteen years of age Graziana looked out on the world through rose-coloured spectacles, even though she considered that she had already been crossed in love.

Harriet drew back from the curb.

'There's no need for you to come with me,' she told the unsmiling man by her side. 'I know my way.'

He held the car door open for her to get in.

'You can't possibly expect me to neglect my duty,' he said. 'I will take you to Anacapri as I have promised, but you need not fear. I have no designs on you, Harriet. Surely you must realise that?'

She stepped back, appalled by the harshness of his tone as he stood waiting for her to obey him, realising that he had told her in as chivalrous a manner as possible that the past was dead and best forgotten.

'Since there is no other way,' she said proudly, taking her place in the passenger seat for the long, nostalgic drive to Sorrento.

Tarquin closed the door behind her, going round to the back of the car to stack her luggage in the trunk, and she sat looking out through the windshield at the familiar Roman scene with her dreams crumbling to pieces in her heart. All around her happy families were meeting and embracing each other and, as they were Italians, the uproar was magnificent. Their high-pitched laughter was something to be envied and the warmth of their loving was everywhere. For a moment she could no longer look at them because their happiness was so great, and then she pushed back the hair which had fallen over her brow and made a new resolution. She must steel herself to meet Tarquin on his own terms, to pretend that the past had been no more than a game to her, too, to smile and look into his eyes with the same indifference which lay coldly in his, since that was what he wanted.

Yet how to do it when every fibre of her being cried out that she was more in love with him now than she had ever been, that the past year had only served to deepen and strengthen her love?

They drove towards Naples along the broad highway which she remembered so well, with the flat coastal plain on one side and the foothills of the Apennines on the other. All along the way the little mountain towns looked down on them, topped by a castle and glittering in the sun as they appeared poised, ready to soar into space, little dream cities of a bygone age which seemed to bear no relation to the present day. Around them, clinging to the foothills, the groves of olives were turned to silver as the light wind stirred their leaves, and everywhere the cypresses, like single brush strokes, marked the horizon.

Tarquin spoke very little, assuming a mask of quiet courtesy which she could not challenge because the change in him was so complete. He was treating her like a stranger, a guest of his grandmother whom he could not ignore without giving offence, but that was all.

Presently he turned the car off the highway.

'You will excuse me,' he said, 'while I collect some cameos? My grandmother is having them re-set at the factory, so you may wish to see the men at work. Afterwards, we must look for somewhere to eat.' He glanced at his watch. 'It is already after twelve o'clock.'

Harriet could not believe that they had been in each other's company for so long, that it was almost three hours since they had met at the airport and that they were still talking as strangers. Looking at his hard profile as he turned the car into the garden of the factory, she thought how much it resembled the old bas-reliefs to be found in this fascinating land, with its high forehead and straight Grecian nose and the firm mouth and chin set in the square-cut jaw. Only the eyes were different, enigmatic grey, English eyes which were a legacy from his father. Otherwise, he was every inch a Roman, tall, elegant and completely self-possessed, although she sought to remember him as he had been only a year ago when they had sailed with the others along the coast to Amalfi with their brown bodies warm in the sun and their hearts as light as the passing wind. What had gone wrong? What had changed him so much? Surely not the gratification of his heart's desire? Her own heart contracted at the thought, yet she could not ask him about Emmy or Carlo or any of the others. To ask would be to know.

They entered the long, cool hall of the factory together, passing into an Aladdin's cave of coral utterly arresting in its magnificence. Glass display cases lined the walls of the central showroom filled with magnificent examples of the carvers' art while the artists themselves sat at benches under the windows, stooped over their meticulous tasks.

Tarquin was recognised immediately. His cameos were ready and would be brought to him at once. The *direttore* hurried away and Harriet moved towards the showcases, fascinated by the items on display as she always was by rare and beautiful pieces of the carver's art.

'This one,' she said impulsively. 'It's the most beautiful thing I've ever seen—so small and delicate, yet so perfect.'

Tarquin came to look over her shoulder and once again she was aware of that strong magnetism which was like a vast, engulfing sea.

'The necklace?' he queried. 'Yes, it is very pretty, but not antique, of course.'

'All the same,' she objected, 'it must be quite valuable. The coral is so beautifully carved.'

'It is darker than it should be,' he decided. 'Perhaps you would like to see how the carving is done?'

He turned towards the benches under the window and she gave the golden chain interspersed with the tiniest cameos she had ever seen a last, lingering look.

The carvers were working on shell, sculpting the lovely profiles of the cameos with tiny blades like scalpels, and she stood entranced, watching as the heads and features took shape as if by magic. It was slow, meticulous work, each man bent low over his particular masterpiece as all his thought and energy was given to the absorbing task. They had probably been making cameos for most of their working lives, for some were old and grey-haired, while others were obviously at the trainee stage, checking, hesitating, paring the shell painstakingly to just the right thickness to obtain the desired result. They did not seem to notice that they were being observed, their eyes and hands steady on their task, and she watched until Tarquin was again standing by her side.

'Time to move on,' he said, 'if we are to catch the ferry.'

She turned reluctantly, smiling up at him.

'It's utterly fascinating,' she said. 'I've never thought of cameos quite in this way before.'

'The corals have become very valuable, especially those that came from the original deposits in the Bay. Now that coral has gone we depend very much on Japan and Australia for our raw material, which is harder and not so good.'

'How about the shell?'

He shrugged.

'That's common and easy enough to come by,' he said. 'The corals I have just collected are almost priceless, by the way, yet my grandmother was wearing them carelessly, without a safety-chain. They were also in need of cleaning.'

Harriet's smile deepened.

'I can imagine!' She had seen the Contessa discard a magnificent emerald ring on a restaurant wash-basin while she dried her hands. 'She values them, but is really very trusting.'

'Too trusting, I think. She values things only for their beauty.' He slipped the white package he had been given into his jacket pocket as they reached the car. 'No doubt that is the best way to appreciate such things.'

'Tarquin,' she asked, 'are you going into the business? On the strictly commercial side,' she added on a dry note.

He smiled down at her.

'You believe me completely materialistic,' he said, 'and perhaps you are right. But the business—no. I cannot imagine myself spending all my days in a Roman *bottega* selling antiques, even at the inflated prices now prevailing on the Via Frattina. Besides, I would be little use at it. I have neither the manner nor the patience to be polite to every passing stranger who wants to dabble in the art.'

'You must be a great disappointment to the Contessa,' she declared spontaneously.

'On the contrary,' he smiled, 'my grandmother is more than pleased with me. I have turned over a new leaf. I am completely settled down.'

With Emmy! Her heart seemed to miss a beat and she could no longer look at him.

'On the estate?' she asked.

'Indeed. I think you will agree that it was my natural habitat. I now administer the estate with the utmost aplomb and make the best wine east of the Abruzzi!'

'You were never one to boast!'

He looked round at her with something in his eyes which she could not fathom.

'I try to tell the truth,' he said. 'Our wine is good. It has sold well for two hundred years and I am only doing what was expected of me. My grandmother was deprived of two sons during the last war, both killed at Cassino, almost on her doorstep, and she was left with three daughters. Two of them emigrated to America with their Italian husbands. There was only my mother left. Her first marriage was a disaster. Julius died tragically of his war wounds in 1944 and she married my father five years later. He was an English businessman, hardly acceptable to the Contessa in those days, but he was her main hope, since the American branch of the family had produced only girls.'

'Graziana,' Harriet murmured.

'Graziana and Sophia and Donna and Bianca,' he added. 'They are all charming, but they were not true heirs, as my grandmother saw them.'

'And you were English—more or less.'

He smiled.

'It took her a long time to get over the fact, even though my mother gave us Roman names, and in spite of the fact that I was her oldest grandson she favoured Angelo most.'

Harriet caught her breath.

'Has Angelo come back?' she asked.

Instantly his expression changed.

'I thought you would have known that,' he said brusquely. 'No, he has not returned, which is a great grief to the Contessa.'

They had reached his car and he opened the door for her. She wanted to ask so much more, but the dark look in his eyes forbade it.

'Thank you,' she said lamely as she settled into the warm

leather seat. 'And thank you for showing me the cameos.'

He dropped a small white package into her lap.

'For old acquaintance's sake,' he said lightly.

'I can't take it!' She pushed the package away.

'You don't know what it is.'

'It's the necklace I admired. Why do you want to give it to me?' She turned to face him. 'You owe me nothing.'

He got in behind the wheel and started the engine.

'As you say.' He kept his gaze on the driveway. 'In that case you can have no valid reason for refusing my gift. You admired it, so I wish to give it to you. That is all.'

'I couldn't wear it!' she declared stormily.

'Can you tell me why?' he queried. 'You said yourself that it was beautiful.'

'Beautiful and very valuable.'

He drove out on to the main road without answering her for a moment.

'I owe you a debt,' he said at last. 'Let me repay it in this way.'

'A debt?'

'You came as soon as my grandmother asked you,' he explained. 'She has been very ill and we have been greatly concerned for her. She has been working too hard and things have been difficult.' He hesitated. 'She longs for peace and Angelo's return.'

'Did she blame me for taking Angelo away?' Harriet asked.

Tarquin's jaw hardened at the question and a spark of anger kindled in his grey eyes, turning them to the colour of steel.

'You must ask her that question yourself,' he said, 'but I hardly think so. Otherwise she would not have asked you to return to your old job.'

A sudden revulsion ran through her at the thought that he might be trying to buy her off, to wipe out the past once and for all.

'I can't take it,' she declared again, looking down at the carefully wrapped box.

For a moment he looked surprised and then he said coldly:

'Why not? It's no more than a token of my gratitude for returning to help my grandmother in an emergency.'

Chilled by the harshness of his tone, she remained silent. Gratitude was a cold word, calculated to hurt, yet not so long ago he had held her in his arms and kissed her in the bright Italian starlight. When she closed her eyes she could remember that kiss, but it could so easily have been just another token of gratitude, his way of saying 'thank you' for the help she had given Emmy in her hour of need— Emmy, who had been Carlo Luciano's wife in these halcyon days when only laughter and sunshine had bounded their horizon!

Tarquin drove towards the coast, and soon they were high on a cliff road with the wide sweep of Naples spread beneath them and the faint outlines of the islands muted by a golden haze. Procida and Ischia were near at hand, but Capri was almost lost to view in the blue of distance. For a moment she could not believe that this magic island was really their destination, that she was going there with Tarquin, of all people, although for him it was merely a duty to be fulfilled. She glanced at the stern profile, at the noble Roman features with the crisp, dark hair growing back from the high forehead and the strong brown hands firm on the steering-wheel. What had he done to her? How had he made it impossible for her to forget?

'Have you ever been to Capri?' he asked, pulling into the driveway of a fabulous hotel which seemed to cling on to the cliff edge by a mere hairsbreadth.

She shook her head.

'Never. I planned to go, of course, but we were generally too busy at the shop. The Contessa used to say that the best time to go was in the spring before the holiday crowds took over.'

It was spring now—early spring, when the whole world was renewing itself, when the carnivals and the flower parades were just beginning and the perfume of orange blossom and bergamot was heavy on the air. The cobalt sea far beneath them, the blue sky far above, the olive groves and the cypresses casting heavy shadows on the warm earth touched her susceptible heart as they had never done before, and even old Vesuvius hovering like a ghost in the background seemed a friendly giant today with not even a puff of smoke rising from his crater to remind them of his propensity for destruction.

Suddenly her spirits soared and she determined to have no more to do with remembering. This was her day and she would live it to the full. She was going to Capri with the man she loved, and if it could only last for twenty-four hours at least it could be perfect.

'We'd better eat before we go down to the ferry,' Tarquin decided, 'and I like this place. Looking over the Bay to Sorrento is an experience in itself, especially as the sun goes down.'

The hotel he had chosen was a modern one, built with the tourist trade in mind, but at this time of year it was practically deserted. Positioned high above the rocks with a wide, colonnaded balcony overhanging the sea, it commanded a view through a group of pines that was truly magnificent. Sheer cliffs fell away at their feet as they stood to look across the Bay to the island where the Contessa was waiting for them while behind them, dazzling in the strong sunlight, a heart-shaped swimming-pool made a blue centrepiece for a dozen or so tables shaded by large sun-umbrellas which immediately suggested a leisurely *aperitivo* before their meal.

While they drank it a table was set for them in the shade of the colonnade and two smiling waiters hovered expectantly, ready to take their order.

'We will no doubt miss the ferry,' Tarquin shrugged, 'but what does it matter? There is always another one.'

He looked down at the sea where the wakes of little steamers plying across the Gulf between Naples and Sorrento broke the blue surface in a pencil line of white, and

somehow he seemed more relaxed, more like the Tarquin
she had known a year ago.

'I'm known here,' he said, 'and the food is invariably
good. I hope you will enjoy it.'

She was going to enjoy everything today, Harriet
thought. Everything he had to offer. Her heart leapt at the
prospect of all these hours which were yet before her and
her cheeks were flushed and her eyes bright as he took his
place opposite to her at the table.

'Order for me,' she suggested. 'I could eat anything today!'

'There will be an organised meal once we reach the
villa,' he mused, glancing through the menu with an expert's eye, 'so I would suggest something light, with a
bottle of the local wine to go with it. You've tried Lacrima
Cristi, of course?'

She shook her head.

'But I will try it now. It is the wine of Vesuvius, isn't it?'

He nodded, giving his order to the waiter who had
greeted him in voluble Italian as if they were old and
trusted friends.

'There's something different about the Campania,' said
Harriet. 'As soon as one reaches Naples the sun seems to
shine more brightly and the people are singing! They don't
appear to have one single care in the world.'

'It is the Italian temperament as opposed to the Roman,'
he answered. 'The Napolitani are the troubadours, the
players of guitars and the singers of songs. No matter how
wretched they are, a song is never far from the surface and
it is always there in their hearts. They have an inbred
gentleness which we in Rome have never possessed.'

She realised how true that was, thinking how easy it
must be to sing when your heart was full of happiness, and
today her own heart seemed to be winging its way to the
heights, over the rocks and the incredibly blue water of the
Gulf towards distant Capri which was her unexpected
destination.

The scampi Tarquin had ordered came in a silver dish
and had been cooked in a rich mushroom sauce, and the

wine they drank with it could have been the nectar of the gods. Lacrima Cristi, Tarquin had called it, and it stood in her glass like bottled sunshine, waiting for her to drink. Beneath them, on the hidden beach, someone was playing a guitar. *Torna a Sorriento!* Return! Return! She had come back, if it was only for a day or even an hour, and she had no regrets.

Her meal ended with a favourite dish, flaming peaches filled with toasted almonds, and she sat back contentedly to watch Tarquin dealing with the generous cheese board which had been brought to him on a little trolley. Unconsciously a sigh escaped her parted lips as she looked beyond his dark head to the shining Campania.

'No wonder Aeneas and his friends fell in love with it on sight,' she mused. 'It's the most beautiful country in the world!'

His eyes clouded at her remark.

'If you don't look too closely,' he said. 'Nothing can be perfect.'

'Perhaps the fault is in ourselves,' she suggested. 'The sun, the sea, the flowers—even the little lizards on the wall —are all quite perfect.'

He rose to his feet, gazing down to the sea.

'Is that what you are looking for?' he asked. 'Perfection in all things?'

'No!' she protested immediately. 'Because it wouldn't make the really happy times stand out, as they always do for me.'

'Such as?' he demanded, coming to stand beside her chair. 'Are we discussing memories?'

'I have many memories of Rome,' she answered quietly.

He looked away from her bright eyes.

'You are lucky,' he said flatly. 'I hope they will increase while you remain there. Did you say that Angelo would return also?'

Harriet felt the hot colour rising in her cheeks.

'I don't know where Angelo is. I thought he might be here.'

His dark eyebrows shot up.

'He left with you, or very soon afterwards,' he said. 'He has not returned.'

It was obvious that he thought she was lying when she denied having seen Angelo during the past year, but she was suddenly too proud to try to convince him otherwise.

'Have we to book on the ferry?' she asked, dismissing his younger brother from the conversation as if Angelo had never had any part in her life, as if he had never tried to play the gay Lothario for want of something better to do. 'It's almost three o'clock.'

'We can go across at five,' he decided. 'Would you like me to drive you to Pompeii while we wait?'

He seemed almost indifferent as to how they spent the rest of the afternoon and she had to swallow her disappointment before she could reply.

'It wouldn't be fair to go there for so short a time,' she decided. 'There's far too much to see and absorb. Besides,' she added deliberately, 'we might miss the ferry and I don't want to keep your grandmother waiting.'

He settled down in his chair again, stretching out his long legs in front of him to enjoy the sun and the last of the wine.

'I take it you would rather stay here and wait for the ferry,' he said lazily.

It suited her very well to relax in the sunshine beside him, to allow time to melt away in the golden haze which crept across the Bay as the sun moved towards the western horizon. Here was peace; here was contentment; here was all that the ancient Greeks had found when they had first discovered Italy!

Then, as if the beauty and the quiet was almost too much to offer to the human mind, pandemonium broke loose. In spite of the fact that the siesta hour was only just ended, a great commotion was taking place in the hall beneath them. Waitresses were scuttling here and there, management was in full voice, and a fleet of cars had arrived at the main entrance.

'A wedding reception, at a reasonable guess,' Tarquin

suggested, getting reluctantly out of his chair. 'Do we retreat while there is still time, or sit it out and hope to be overlooked?'

'I've never seen an Italian wedding.' Harriet's eyes were sparkling. 'I'd like to stay.'

They looked down from their vantage point on the upper terrace while the guests assembled, and later, when the bride and groom led them in to the wedding breakfast, Harriet hung over the iron balustrade to obtain a better view. The bride was very young, probably still in her teens, and the bridegroom a smiling, dark-haired youth who stood beside his wife of two hours with an air of quiet possessiveness, half shy, half arrogant in his new-found manhood while all his numerous family and his new in-laws formed a happy crowd around them.

In spite of the initial noise and excitement it was a fairly formal reception and a very pretty one. The bride, in her simple white dress and traditional lace veil, was obviously beloved by all, and Mamma and Papa did the honours with a great show of pride in their offspring. When the time came for the young couple to go off on their own an elaborate gilt trolley, probably kept by the hotel for the purpose, was wheeled into the lounge. It was stacked high with gift-wrapped parcels, one for each guest in appreciation of their presence there at an only daughter's marriage to the man she loved.

Tarquin paused in the hall as they went down, waiting for his bill, and Harriet moved a little nearer to the happy scene in the open lounge. The bride, attended by her bridesmaids, was moving among the guests with baskets of linen handkerchiefs all beautifully hand-embroidered and nestling in the baskets like delicate butterflies, some decorating the handles, as if they were only resting there in passing. When all the guests had received one, the little bride turned shyly to Harriet, proffering her basket.

'You will take one?' she asked, smiling in Tarquin's direction. 'It is for happiness and the gift of love in marriage.'

How could she possibly refuse? Harriet thanked the little bride in her halting Italian.

'What have you got?' Tarquin enquired at her elbow.

Harriet's fingers trembled as they fastened over her unexpected gift.

'The wedding almonds,' she said. 'Aren't they called *confetti*? It was a very kind thing for her to do. I want to thank her personally and wish them both happiness.'

She pushed her way through the crowd while he stood watching with an odd smile on his lips.

'Well?' he asked when she finally returned to his side. 'Is your conscience quite clean now?'

'I'm not quite sure what you mean.' She followed him out to the car.

'Accepting something you haven't earned, like the necklace,' he said.

'This was quite different.' She looked down at the tiny posy of flowers nestling in the white folds of the handkerchief. 'It was given in happiness.'

'Aren't you going to open it?' he asked, driving away.

'Yes, in a minute.'

She sat clasping the wedding gift in her hands, aware of his nearness and all the love and happiness they had left behind them in the hotel lounge. Then, determinedly, she unfastened the colourful little nosegay to count out the almonds.

'One for health,' she said, 'and one for wealth; one for peace and contentment, one for happiness and—one for love in marriage.'

The tears were too near her eyes for her to look at him, but she knew that there was no response in him as he gazed steadily along the way ahead.

They boarded the ferry for Capri as the sun sank towards the sea and the old magic stirred in her heart again. Tarquin stood against the rail, his back to the land where lights were already pricking out along the coastline, and Harriet leaned beside him, dangerously near in the romantic dusk. A little wind straying over the Sorrento peninsula hurried to meet them and suddenly all the sea and the sky and the distant mainland hills were aflame with the richness of the sunset. It plunged Capri into darkness for a moment until all the colour rose behind her own mountains to bathe the magic isle in fiery light.

'It's more wonderful than I imagined,' she confessed. 'I should have come here long ago.'

She had seen the island, of course, from a distance when Angelo had rushed her round the precarious scenic road to Positano on the back of his motor-scooter, but the shadowy island on the western horizon had remained a mystery to her. It was strange and heartrending to be going there for the first time with Tarquin, as she was going now, but she told herself again that she had no regrets.

They spoke very little during the crossing, looking down at the sea till he asked her if she would like anything more to eat.

'Not one bite,' she assured him, coming out of her reverie. 'Cream cakes would only spoil the memory of a perfect lunch, and you did say your grandmother would have a meal prepared for us.'

'She eats late, as you know,' he answered, 'but it will be worth waiting for!'

As they approached the island she could see how precipitous the cliffs were and how steep the way would be to Anacapri right at the top. It was crowned by sunlight, while Capri itself lay in deepest shadow, a blue island rising straight out of the sea with a halo on its head. No wonder a sad and disillusioned old Roman emperor had chosen it as his home for the last eleven years of his life!

Towering above them, the sombre outline of Monte Solaro with its sheer crags and inaccessible cliffs seemed almost hostile for a moment until someone on the deck beneath them started to sing. The rich, vibrant notes of a Neapolitan love-song sped out across the water, warming her susceptible heart as she clung to the rail with an added awareness of the beauty all around her. The blue isle which was Capri came nearer and nearer until she could make out the marina and the rows of ferry-boats moored beside the quay with all the fussy small craft bobbing up and down on the tide. The church bells rang out *Ave Maria* in the arrested dusk as they reached the shore and Tarquin put his hand under her elbow to help her over the gangway.

On shore they were greeted with cries of 'Taxi!' 'Taxi!' until he finally hired a suitable car. He had left his own at Sorrento to be picked up on his return for the journey back to Rome. On the beach the local fishermen were gathered around the launches from the Blue Grotto, while a straggling line of little donkeys with bent heads and drooping ears stood, deep in thought, at the water's edge.

Their taxi-driver was young and talkative, evidently recognising Tarquin from earlier visits to the island and eager to acquaint him with the latest news of his grandmother.

'*La Contessa*, she is most well,' he declared. 'I see her to-day on a stick, walking with her dog. She go a little way along the road from the villa where there is not much traffic just now.'

Tarquin frowned.

'I did not expect her to be out walking,' he said, 'even with the aid of a stick. I trust you drove carefully, Mario, when you passed her.'

Oh, he had gone more than carefully, Mario declared. He had even stopped altogether to let *la Contessa* pass him with safety and the little dog had barked at him, but only with happiness, of course!

They drove through the Piazza as the rusty bells of the campanile were ringing six o'clock and Mario swung the car at what seemed to be a reckless speed round the first bend of the scenic road which led to Anacapri. Creeper-covered villas and grand hotels and restaurants slid away behind them, leaving Capri and its campanile in the blue-grey haze of the evening far below. Up and up they went on the narrow road, negotiating its hairpin bends as Mario chattered incessantly behind the wheel. At the very top of the island the sun still lingered, as if loath to leave the little villas of Anacapri behind, and Mario turned the car along a still narrower road to their destination, a lovely, silent villa on the edge of the cliff. It stood back from the road in a beautiful garden surrounded by a long pergola, a house open to sun and wind and the gentle voice of the sea, like a Greek temple. There was light everywhere between the columns of white marble which supported loggias and arcades, and little marble benches under the cypresses to sit on, and a vineyard sloping precariously back down the hill.

An owl rose on noiseless wings from a dark corner as the car drew up and all at once the inner courtyard was flooded with artificial light. Under the lantern in the villa doorway stood the Contessa, a striking figure in a long grey gown leaning heavily on a silver-headed walking-stick. In spite of her great age her hair was still black and plentiful, worn in two loose folds, like wings, on either side of her face, and her high forehead above the straight Grecian nose was like alabaster. The years had hollowed her cheeks a little, but no passage of time or conflict with grief could have altered that firm mouth and determined chin.

'Harriet!' she said with just the faintest hint of reserve in her deep voice, 'I am glad that you have come so quickly.'

'I knew you neded me.' Harriet took the proffered hand, feeling the older woman's fingers cold to her touch. 'I hope you are now fully recovered?'

'Almost.' The Contessa's dark eyes searched her face, the penetrating gaze going deep. 'You have come alone?'

Harriet's heart began to beat so violently that she could hardly speak. She knew that the Contessa was thinking about Angelo.

'Quite alone,' she said as Tarquin came round the car with Mario and the luggage. 'It's beautiful here,' she added lamely.

Renata de Filippo looked into the gathering dusk.

'Anacapri is a refuge I have known for many years,' she said. 'It is a place of peace at this time of year and very beautiful. You will stay, of course, for a day or two? We have much to discuss?'

'You're very kind,' Harriet said, glancing at the silent Tarquin, 'but I think I should return to Rome as quickly as possible. I understand you've had to close the shop.'

Her hostess turned to lead the way inside.

'That was inevitable. You see, there was no one I could fully trust when I was not able to be there myself,' she explained. 'It is difficult to find conscientious people nowadays with the knowledge I require.'

Following close behind her, Harriet wondered if that was the only reason for the Contessa's swift summons, and the name of Angelo echoed painfully in her ears. Could it be that Renata de Filippo believed that they were still seeing each other and this was her way of regaining contact with her beloved grandson?

Suddenly she found herself gazing up into two piercing grey eyes. Tarquin had deposited her luggage at the foot of the spiral staircase to await his grandmother's instructions and there was cold accusation in the look he gave her. He, too, thought that she had seen Angelo frequently during the past year, although he had refused to pass judgment on his grandmother's reaction when they had first spoken about Angelo. Perhaps the Contessa was ready to denounce her, or was she just hoping, deep in her heart, that her presence in Rome would bring Angelo back?

Following Tarquin up the winding marble staircase Harriet did not know what to think. They had left the Contessa in the circular hallway, leaning heavily on her stick, but she knew that the old lady was watching them closely as they reached the landing above.

'You have been put in the west room,' Tarquin told her. 'It has the best view of the bay and most of the sunshine.'

He led the way along the upstairs corridor with familiar ease, depositing her luggage at the half open door of a bedroom where the lights were already on.

'Rosina will come to help you unpack,' he said, halting

in the doorway. 'I hope you will be comfortable. As my grandmother says, this is the finest view in Anacapri and you will get all the morning sun.'

Harriet looked beyond him into the lovely room, at the gleaming mosaic floor with its scattered, hand-made rugs and the carved posters of the single bed matching the heavy old Italian furniture which looked so well against the stark white-painted walls, and suddenly she wished that she could have felt that she had come home. The villa was only a rented house, however, and soon even the Contessa would leave it to the silence of the moutains to return to Rome.

Tarquin picked up her suitcases to carry them to the luggage-rack beside the window.

'If there's anything else you need,' he said, 'you must ask Rosina.'

There was nothing else she wanted in a material sense, but her eyes were suddenly misted by tears.

'Tarquin,' she asked, 'do you think I should have come?'

He took a full minute to answer her, hesitating as if he was not quite sure what to say in the circumstances, his manner still coolly aloof as he searched her upturned face.

'You know the answer to that better than I do,' he said brusquely. 'If you have come solely to please my grand-mother you must tell her so, but remember, she is too old and too wise to be fobbed off with half a truth.'

He still did not trust her. He had only listened with half an ear to what she had to say about Angelo, but after all, it could not concern him very much whether she was in love with Angelo or not.

Turning to the window, she heard him go back down the uncarpeted stairs to where his grandmother was waiting.

CHAPTER TWO

WHEN Rosina had helped her to unpack and hang up her dresses in the capacious wardrobe which stood against one wall, Harriet bathed in the deep marble bath in the adjoining room while the fiery little Italian girl sang blithely to the accompaniment of the running water.

'*Bella, bella Margherita!*' chanted Rosina, selecting a suitable dress for Harriet to wear for the remainder of the evening. 'This one I like! You will wear it to please the *signorino*, yes?'

How could it please Tarquin when his thoughts were so obviously elsewhere? Harriet held up the green dress with its tiered chiffon skirt which complemented her fair skin and red-gold hair. It was the colour of the sea in quiet places and it also matched her eyes which were her finest feature, green eyes with a fleck of gold in them like sunlight.

When she went slowly downstairs it was to find Tarquin alone in the little *sala* whose windows stood wide open to the night. She came up behind him in her soft evening slippers so that he did not seem to notice, and she saw how hard his mouth was in the reflected light from the terrace and how his hands were thrust deeply into the pockets of his white evening jacket as if he was trying his best to control a surge of feeling which he could not understand. Beyond him, riding the dark sky, a full moon had paled the stars into insignificance and the rocks dropped steeply away to the beach of Tiberio far below. Punta Serina stood out sharply into the sea, with the entrance to the fabled Blue Grotto somewhere beyond it, and she wondered if she would ever go there to see the fantastic blue light and listen to the echo of the boatmen singing their traditional love-songs in the eerie stillness.

'My grandmother has asked me to stay for a few days to take you back to Rome,' Tarquin said without turning. 'Monday is a holiday. Will you be ready to leave early on Tuesday morning?'

He seemed impatient to return to Rome, although he had said that he would never want to live there.

'If you would rather go back earlier, I can find my own way,' she suggested. 'There are good bus and rail connections from Sorrento.'

He moved abruptly, turning to look at her at last.

'I have a great deal of work to do,' he said briefly. 'The estate is now my sole responsibility and the new vines must be attended to. There is also Emmy,' he added. 'We must make a journey to Florence as soon as possible.'

Emmy! Her heart contracted at the thought of Emmy, who had been Carlo Luciano's wife and was now his widow.

'Really, Tarquin, you mustn't worry about me,' she protested. 'I realise that you have—other commitments and I can easily look after myself.'

He glanced down at her with a vague contradiction in his eyes before they hardened perceptibly.

'I'm sure you can,' he said coldly. 'My grandmother and I have business to discuss, however—estate business—and it is easier for us to talk here than over the telephone. Anacapri is quiet at this time of the year, but I'm sure you will find plenty of interest to take up your attention. I will put a car at your disposal—probably Mario's taxi—and you can tour the island and patronise all the expensive shops.'

'That's something I *won't* be able to afford,' she smiled. 'I've come prepared to work, Tarquin, but this lovely trip to Capri is an extra bonus. I'd like best to go to San Michele and perhaps Mario could take me there.'

'It's no more than a stone's throw from where we are now,' he said, moving away from the window. 'If you're quite determined to go we could walk.'

That brief, unconsidered 'we' rang in her heart like a

joyful bell as they were joined by the Contessa moving like a pale ghost across the room.

'We will go out to the terrace and perhaps dine there,' she suggested. 'I want to hear all the news of Rome, Tarquin, and what you have been doing at Cerano. I hear that you're making much of the estate these days and that it is almost returned to its former grandeur.'

'It's paying its way,' Tarquin agreed, following them out to the moonlit terrace where he poured their wine from a silver goblet into the three beautiful Venetian glasses which Rosina had placed ready on a tray. 'I've some way to go yet before we will be showing a profit, I'm afraid.'

'One must start slowly,' the Contessa said. 'There are no short cuts to proficiency, but you will do well, Tarquin, once you can give your whole attention to the estate. It has been sadly neglected in the past because I had no heart for administration on so grand a scale after your father died and, of course, you and Angelo had to be educated. However, now——' She paused to give him a long, calculating look. 'Now things could be different,' she concluded firmly. 'Perhaps I shall live to see you settled at Cerano and happily married.'

So they weren't married! Emmy was not yet Tarquin's wife. A mad, wild delight flooded into Harriet's heart only to be immediately quenched by the look in Tarquin's eyes.

'I have no thought of marrying at present,' he said coldly. 'Other things must come first.'

'Do not wait too long,' advised the Contessa. 'The years go by so quickly, with so much to do, and there is no substitute for happiness. Marital happiness is the world's greatest joy, I can assure you. I knew it once and it has warmed my heart ever since.'

Harriet thought of the wedding almonds, the *confetti* which she had been given by a stranger to wish her well in the moment of her own happiness in the Sorrento hotel.

It was warm enough to dine outside, the Contessa decided when they had drunk a second glass of wine, and Rosina prepared the table in a sheltered corner of the loggia, lighting small pink candles in little alabaster holders to place on either side of the bowl of honeysuckle and roses which she had arranged as a centrepiece. Young vines drooped from the pergola, sheltering them from any truant breeze that might come straying in from the sea, and the cypresses stood like dark sentinels in the background guarding their privacy as the moon rose like a great lantern to stand arrrested above the Villa Jovis and the Bay. It was a night of pure magic which Harriet knew she would never forget although her uncertain heart was so close to despair. A flask of rose-coloured wine on a marble table, a bunch of flowers in an alabaster bowl, candlelight paled by the full brilliance of the moon, and a man and a woman sitting face to face in the warm night air! The Contessa was there, too, but she seemed to have faded into the shadows, a grey ghost against the pale marble of the loggia contemplating the prospect of the future while she watched.

When the meal was finished she excused herself, saying that she had had a busy day.

'Tomorrow Tarquin must take you on a tour of the island,' she suggested. 'You must not miss seeing Capri at its best.'

'How long will you stay here?' Harriet asked.

'Not too long,' her employer decided. 'I have much to do in Rome when the time comes, and Capri gets overcrowded during the summer months. It is also much too warm for my liking. I may go to the mountains. I do not know, but first I will establish you in the Via Frattina so that you can report to me from time to time. You will soon pick up the threads of the business again because it is something you always wanted to do.'

The warmth of feeling which had always existed between them seemed to be renewed in spite of that initial hesitation when they had first met and Harriet rose to follow her from the room.

'Goodnight, Tarquin,' she said as he held open the door for her to re-enter the *sala*. 'And—thank you for bringing me.'

Tarquin escorted them to the foot of the stairs.

'You should be sleeping down here,' he said to his grandmother. 'I'm surprised that you haven't thought of it.'

'I must be able to move around, even if it is with the help of a stick,' the Contessa replied. 'I spent four whole weeks in my bedroom when I first came here, but now I see the stairs as my first real challenge. I'm determined to manage them—on my own.

'Tarquin tries to bully me,' she declared while he stood below in the hall watching her uncertain progress as she negotiated the staircase leaning heavily on Harriet's arm, 'but really we see eye to eye about most things. He has made a great success of the estate since he took over, which makes me very proud of him. The wine we make is one of the finest in the whole district, but unfortunately many of the vines were destroyed some years ago and never replaced. Tarquin has now undertaken this task and is making a great success of it. Of course, he will own the estate one day. There is no one else.'

She had not mentioned Angelo this time and Harriet would not distress her by asking questions.

'Tarquin has stepped so naturally into the position of power,' the old lady reflected, 'and taken over all my family responsibilities. I could not do without him. As for the rumours you may hear about him, take no notice of them. Rome could not exist for very long without a scandal of one sort or another!'

She paused at the door of her bedroom, taking her hand from Harriet's arm.

'It is my wish,' she said, 'that he should marry, and that is part of the reason why I have sent for you. At present too much of his time is taken up by Emmy Luciano and I do not like the idea. A new face on the Roman scene might help to distract his attention from his friend's wife.'

'Surely—his widow,' Harriet suggested. 'Carlo drowned that night when we were all at Amalfi. I shall never forget it because it was all so sudden. One moment we were in the boat, singing and laughing because we were so happy, and then, in a split second, it was all changed. That awful wind blew up and we were in difficulty. Carlo Luciano and Emmy and Angelo were in the first boat and it overturned so quickly. I don't think Carlo was a strong swimmer, and certainly Emmy wasn't. She seemed to panic——'

The Contessa stiffened where she stood.

'You must not think about it,' she advised harshly. 'It is in the past, and no one can blame Tarquin for rescuing Emmy instead of her husband. No one really knows what happened that night except Angelo.'

She opened the door and went into her room, closing it firmly between them.

That was to be all, Harriet realised. No further questions, no probing into the aftermath of that fatal night was to be tolerated, now or ever.

The certain hardness which she had always recognised as part of Renata de Filippo's make-up had shown on the surface for a moment and instantly she was reminded of the new Tarquin who had replaced the generous one she had known. He seemed to stand above her, aloof, disturbing and commanding in his new role of *padrone* of the family estate, tearing her heart to shreds.

She saw him once again that night, standing at the edge of the moon-blanched terrace staring out to sea, and even from the distance of her balcony window she could imagine how hard his face was, how implacable his resolve to go his own way.

Almost against her better judgment, she promised to manage the shop in the Via Frattina until she was no longer needed.

'I'll stay for six months,' she told the Contessa the following morning when she carried up her breakfast tray. 'It will give you time to get well.'

'We shall see,' said her employer. 'A great deal can happen in six months, especially in Rome.'

True to his promise Tarquin was waiting for her when she carried his grandmother's tray down the spiral staircase to the hall where Rosina rushed to relieve her of her burden.

'*Signorina*, no!' she exclaimed. 'It is I who must carry

the tray! You must go to walk with the *signorino* and not keep him waiting!'

Already the romantic Italian girl had dreamed up a fine romance between them and could hardly restrain her curiosity as they walked away. Why, she wondered, did they not go arm-in-arm, as lovers should? They were going to San Michele, the most romantic place on the whole island, where a golden oriole would sing to them from a fig tree and little green lizards would slink away between the stones at their approach. They would be able to see all of Capri from that wonderful place and sit on a marble bench under a cypress to kiss when no one was looking! Yes, they were a handsome couple, the young master and the lady *inglese* who had come such a long way to help the Contessa in her hour of need. Rosina had never been to London herself, but she understood that it was a city as large as Rome. Come to think of it, she had never been to Rome, either!

Tarquin took Harriet's arm to guide her across the narrow road and suddenly she felt the full warmth of the morning sunshine on her skin like a benediction, the blaze of it dazzling her eyes.

The sky overhead was blue, like a sapphire, and the heady scent of orange blossom filled the air. Some of the orchard trees had kept their fruit and they hung like golden lanterns over the moss-covered walls which bounded the roadway. Lemons gleamed palely under their protective pergolas and birds were singing in every tree.

The birds came in early spring in their thousands, Tarquin explained as they took the narrower road to Axel Munthe's villa. Thrushes, turtledoves, skylarks, nightingales and swallows, to say nothing of the wagtails and chaffinches and waders.

'It takes about six weeks for them all to pass over,' he added. 'Perhaps the wild geese are the most spectacular. I have seen the whole sky dark with them flying in strict formation.'

'Winging their way to Britain!' Harriet mused.

He looked down at her.

'Will you do that when my grandmother is well enough to cope with the shop on her own?' he asked. 'Wing your way back to London?'

Harriet drew in a deep breath. It could be no more than a conventional question, but she had to answer it with truth.

'I didn't make any definite plans to return and I have just told the Contessa that I'll stay for at least six months until she is fully recovered.'

Unlike his grandmother, he did not say that a good deal could happen in the course of six months. Instead he pointed to the cliff above them where San Michele stood, riveted to the rock face and gleaming in the morning sun.

'It's beautiful!' she cried when she could find words to express her thoughts. 'One man's dream come miraculously true.'

'He had to work for it,' Tarquin said practically, 'and he paid the price of blindness in the end.'

Harriet wondered if there was always a price to be paid for happiness or achievement as she followed him to the villa which had been no more than a ruined chapel when the Swedish doctor first discovered it.

An old woman in a black dress and shiny black apron gave them good-morning, looking after them with kindly curiosity as they went on their way.

'What do you want to see?' Tarquin asked.

'Everything! But especially the garden where he spent so much of his time in the sun. I never thought that I would one day sit there,' Harriet confessed.

They went quickly through the house and out to a terraced garden all ablaze with sun. It was deserted at that early hour and they had it to themselves as they walked the winding pathways through avenues of cypresses and columns of priceless marble garlanded with vines and honeysuckle. Jewel-bright flowers grew everywhere, and all the birds in Anacapri seemed to be singing in the trees. It was a moment to cherish, a moment to keep in her heart for ever.

They walked to the end of the terrace to look down into the clear depths of the sea a thousand feet below and suddenly it seemed to Harriet as if a cloud had obscured the sun. Staring down at the cruel rocks far beneath them, she was transported back in memory to that terrible day when she had stood on the cliff above similar rocks at Amalfi and watched Tarquin helping a weeping Emmy to safety. He had taken Carlo's wife in his arms with the utmost tenderness, kissing her hair in a brief gesture of pity and love.

'Don't look down if it affects you,' he advised at her side. 'If you look out across the bay you will see all of Naples and Ischia and Procida over to the left. Vesuvius is just coming out of the haze, and Sorrento is practically straight ahead.'

His prosaic tone and the panorama unfolding before her eager gaze recalled her to the present. Amalfi and all it stood for was in the past while today, at least, was hers.

They sat on a little bench beneath a marble pergola, watching the antics of a green lizard playing under a rosemary bush, its lustrous, inquisitive eyes full upon them as it panted in the heat. The garden with its pools of subdued light between the cypresses was suddenly a place of haunting mystery and Tarquin seemed willing to walk with her into the distant past, which had no connection with Amalfi.

'What kind of man do you think Tiberius was?' she asked after a moment's thought. 'He built villas all over Capri, and when he died his friends and enemies cast them over the precipices into the sea because they misjudged him.'

'A very disillusioned one.' His tone was dry. 'He had done his best, to no avail. He might also have felt frustrated by a set of circumstances over which he had no control. Rome was a hotbed of gossip and intrigue in those days, as it is now.'

She bit her lip, remembering what his grandmother had said about the scandal which had rocked the Eternal City for a day or two and was surely now forgotten, but when she looked at her companion's stern profile she knew that Tarquin would not easily forget. He would resent the gossip more for Emmy's sake than for his own.

But no more of Emmy for today! The sky above them was a cloudless blue and the sea below stretched, calm and waveless, to the mainland shore where the Sorrento peninsula slept lazily in the sun. Vesuvius had taken shape as a shadowy cone in the background and the island peaks of Solaro and Tiberio were etched clearly against the horizon. Tarquin glanced at his watch.

'Mario will be here with the car by now,' he said. 'I have hired it for the day.'

They took the precipitous road down to Capri, with Mario singing at the wheel. At a junction of two roads, however, he left them, saying that he would go on to Capri to enquire about his sister, who was ill. He explained that he had five sisters and two brothers living on the island, and two were in heaven. They were a happy, united family, and he could not fail to say mass for the *bimba*, who was the youngest of them all.

Tarquin took over the wheel and their day began. The ancient 'island of the goats' was sheer magic. They drove along the high side of a valley and down the winding road to Marina Piccola to walk, like Augustus in his famous gardens at the foot of towering Certosa; they lingered in the church in the square and went on foot a little way up the mountain for a better view; they sat out the siesta hour on the terrace of a restaurant poised like an eagle's nest on the edge of a cliff, drinking a bottle of the local wine with their bread and *caccia cavalla*, which Tarquin said was the best cheese on the island, and finally they took the Via Tiberio to that other mountain where an emperor had lived in austere solitude two thousand years ago after he had turned his back on Rome.

It seemed to Harriet that her companion was entering quite willingly into her spirit of adventure. He had a deep knowledge of the island's history and a fund of legend to draw on to keep her interested. This was the Tarquin she remembered, so what could have happened to change him so much? Today he seemed to have set aside the reserve with which he had met her at the airport as easily as he had discarded the conventional city suit he had worn, looking relaxed and almost happy with his strong chest bared to the sun and the wind in his hair. Leading the way up the path to the cliff top or helping her to climb back down again, he seemed younger than he had ever been in the past, casting the burden of his responsibilities aside for a few hours, at least.

When the sun finally set towards the west there were bells everywhere. The whole island seemed full of the sound of them as it drifted upwards in the warm air to where they stood on the edge of a vineyard overlooking the sea. Soon it would be time to go back to the villa where the Contessa would be waiting for them. Impulsively Harriet stopped to pick her some of the tiny purple orchids which sprang out of the sweet-scented grass at the edge of the path and soon her hands were full of flowers. Anemones, crocuses and wild hyacinths were soon added to her bouquet while Tarquin looked on with an indulgent smile curving his hard mouth and an odd expression in his eyes.

'You are like a small child at her first picnic,' he observed. 'There are plenty of flowers in the villa garden.'

'But not like these! Don't spoil it for me, Tarquin,' she begged. 'Not today.'

He came up behind her without answering to stand there for a moment while she arranged the flowers into a nosegay, and suddenly an errant little wind from the distant Bay blew a strand of her hair across his cheek. She turned, sweeping it back from her brow, and almost instantly she was in his arms.

The kiss he gave her seemed to last for an eternity, a harsh, demanding kiss which swept away the present in a fierce memory of the past until, just as suddenly as he had taken her, he let her go.

'We are going to be late,' he said briefly, his eyes more

coldly grey than they had been in Rome. 'My grandmother doesn't like to be kept waiting.'

Harriet followed him back down the path with the scent of myrtle in her nostrils and the gold of the *ginestra* like a haze before her tear-filled eyes. Anyone might have kissed her at the end of such a day, but not like that. Not defiantly, harshly, as if to prove to her that the past no longer mattered between them.

The bells were ringing the Angelus as they reached the villa where the Contessa was waiting. She accepted the nosegay Harriet had picked for her, arranging the flowers in a lustre jar on a table beside her favourite chair, but not before she had given them both a long, searching scrutiny, as if she would probe deeply into the secret places of their hearts. Unsatisfied, she turned away.

'We will talk of Rome,' she said, walking ahead of them into the long dining-room where their supper was set. 'I wish to open the shop again at once, but there is much to do.'

'Let me go back straight away,' Harriet suggested, knowing that she could not stay even on this enchanted isle, with or without Tarquin. 'It is a holiday tomorrow, but I could go over the stock and generally get the shop in order so that we could open the following day.'

Renata de Filippo took her place at the head of the long refectory table.

'Where will you stay?' she asked.

'I thought I might be able to get into one of the smaller hotels,' Harriet answered. 'Somewhere near to the shop so that I can walk there rather than use the buses.'

'They are always overcrowded at the rush hour,' the Contessa agreed rather vaguely. 'Or so I understand. And taxis are impossible. Not only do they charge exorbitant prices but they get into the same traffic jams as the buses and are just a waste of money.' She considered the situation while she applied herself to her soup. 'Graziana has a flat quite near the Piazza di Spagna which would be ideal,' she decided as Rosina cleared away the used plates. 'She shared it with a fellow student for some time, but the girl moved out recently. I understand she got married instead of going on with her studies. Young women have no sense nowadays!'

'Graziana may not want to share again,' Harriet protested, remembering the faint hesitation in Graziana's welcome at the airport.

'Considering that I am paying her rent, she has very little choice,' the Contessa declared. 'It will be an excellent arrangement for you both. Don't you think so, Tarquin?'

'I am not competent to pass an opinion.' Tarquin rose to pour their wine, his manner determinedly aloof. 'We must allow Graziana and Harriet to choose for themselves.'

'Certainly,' his grandmother agreed, 'but a word of advice never comes amiss and at least we know Harriet's background.'

It was left to Harriet to make her own arrangements with Graziana if she wished and the following morning she set sail for Sorrento again with Tarquin by her side. She had been on Capri for less than forty-eight hours, but it had seemed like a lifetime. She might never see its white villas and towering cliffs again, but she would always remember the scent of honeysuckle and roses and see a tiny lizard basking in the sun on a marble loggia surrounded by flowers. She would hear the song of the nightingale as it hid in a peach tree and the silver voices of bells as they rang through the sweet-scented air, and she would see all the warmth of the sun caught in a glass of *vino bianco* and the shadows gathering under a marble pergola when the day was done.

At Sorrento Tarquin took his car from the garage where he had left it, glancing at his watch to discover that it was again time to eat.

'We'll go up to the President,' he suggested.

Not back to the same hotel where they had dined before and Harriet had been given the gift of *confetti* from a happy bride!

They ate their simple meal on a high terrace overlooking

the Gulf where they could look down on the blue water criss-crossed by the white wakes of the ferries hurrying back to Capri. Beneath them Sorrento spread like a multi-coloured carpet, its trees and red rooftops tumbling to the water's edge.

'If you would rather not go all the way to Rome I could catch a train from Naples,' Harriet offered.

'And get caught up in the holiday rush?' He shook his head. 'No, Harriet, I will see you back to Rome and perhaps I will stay there for a day or two to help you re-open the shop.'

'But you don't like that sort of work,' she protested. 'You would much rather be at Cerano. You said so.'

He frowned.

'I won't deny it,' he agreed, 'but I have a duty to see you safely settled in Rome.'

He was taking her back to the Eternal City only because of the promise he had made to his grandmother. She turned to him angrily.

'I'm not a child,' she protested, 'though you chose to call me one yesterday when I was picking the Contessa's flowers! She did seem to appreciate them, though, and I'm glad I took them back for her.' Suddenly she remembered how crushed her little nosegay had looked after Tarquin had kissed her. 'Of course it was a childish gesture,' she added, managing to steady her voice, 'but it was one I wanted to make. She has been very kind to me and—I appreciate the fact.'

'My grandmother is a very shrewd lady,' he answered mildly. 'She will have assessed you carefully, otherwise she would not have sent for you. My one idea in coming back to Rome with you is to make quite sure that everything goes smoothly when you open the shop for her.'

There was nothing personal about his desire to help her, nothing to be suggested by that solitary, devastating kiss out there on the headland at Anacapri with the scent of myrtle in the air and the deep blue lithospermum at their feet.

They were in Rome by nightfall, driving through the

crowded streets in their quest for Graziana. A slight rain had begun to fall as they reached the Piazza di Spagna and turned into one of the side streets bordering the square.

'It's somewhere here,' Tarquin remembered. 'Number twenty-four.'

Graziana was more than surprised to see them. She was preparing to go out to a party.

'I didn't expect you back so soon,' she said frankly, looking from one of them to the other. 'What happened?'

'Nothing out of the ordinary,' Tarquin assured her, seating himself on her rickety sofa with his long legs stretched out before him. 'We need a roof over our heads, though. Can you put Harriet up for a day or two while she looks for a suitable hotel?'

Graziana hesitated.

'Sure,' she said almost reluctantly. 'You know I have the extra bed.'

'It may only be for a couple of nights,' Harriet explained awkwardly. 'I'll get my bearings tomorrow and see what I can find.'

Tarquin was looking fixedly at his cousin.

'Grandmother thought you might like some company,' he suggested. 'Harriet and you used to get on quite well together.'

'Sure we did,' said Graziana carefully. 'What makes you think anything might have changed?'

She was suddenly on the defensive, the hard-boiled American girl making her own decision about the future, and Harriet wondered what she had to hide. A secret love affair, perhaps, or just the straightforward desire to live alone?

'I promise I won't move in on you permanently,' she said, 'if you really mean to have me for a few days.'

'A few days—a week—what does it matter?' Graziana tossed the dark hair back from her forehead with a quick movement which appeared to cancel all argument. 'As Tarquin has just pointed out, we got on very well last time around, so why not now? You're welcome to my poor abode, if you can put up with my untidiness. I warn you, though, that I step out of everything and leave it on the floor when it suits me. It's my hideous American upbringing, you see, and just one of the things that make my grandmother writhe!'

'Graz!' Harriet laughed, 'I'm sure we'll make it.'

Graziana looked across the room at Tarquin.

'And what about you, my dear cousin?' she enquired. 'Are you prepared to sleep on my couch all night or will you be hot-footing it back to Cerano in search of solace now that you have Harri nicely settled in?'

'Couches are not in my line.' Tarquin rose to stretch his legs, prowling to the window to look out on the trees of the Villa Borghese above the opposite rooftops. 'I'll be at the Vittoria as usual, I expect.'

'And then back to the glorious freedom of the estate,' Graziana suggested dryly. 'Haven't we enough wine as it is?'

'Not nearly enough,' he assured her reasonably, 'but I will send you a bottle or two when I get back to entertain your university friends, if you wish.'

Graziana frowned.

'We can't afford a taste for your exclusive vintages,' she retorted. 'All we can drink is plonk. Send the wine to Harriet, if you must.'

'You are in a difficult mood tonight,' Tarquin reflected, 'so I will make myself scarce. I have quite a lot to do. Will you be at the shop tomorrow as early as possible?' he asked, turning to Harriet on his way to the door. 'We have a lot of stock to check and I would like to get back to Cerano by Thursday.'

'Because of Emmy!' Graziana said as soon as he had closed the flat door between them. 'He took Emmy to Cerano after Carlo's death—after you left.'

Harriet's heart contracted with sudden pain.

'It's something we have no right to speak about,' she said.

'Why not?' Graziana strolled to the kitchen door. 'Half

of Rome is talking about it and I guess I have a right. I'm family. I wasn't there, of course, so I don't know all the grisly details, but I do know that Tarquin blames himself in some way. He was older than any of you and he considered himself responsible, but how could he be responsible for an accident? Emmy panicked when the boat overturned and Tarquin was there to save her, that was all. He might have saved Carlo, too, but that's hardly the point. He didn't and Carlo drowned. It's as simple as that. Or isn't it?' she demanded when Harriet did not answer her immediately. 'You know that Carlo's body wasn't found, of course?'

'No, I didn't know.'

'It could have been swept into some underwater cavern,' Graziana reasoned. 'You know what the tides are like along that coast. Nobody can really say, and with the lack of reliable information rumour multiplies, I guess. One day Carlo will be found and then it will all be raked up again, to Tarquin's sorrow.'

'They were friends,' Harriet pointed out. 'But don't let's talk about it any more.'

'Emmy was always eager to have two strings to her bow,' Graziana mused. 'Are you hungry?' she added, switching the conversation dramatically. 'I'm not a good cook, but I could rustle up something with eggs.'

'I thought you were going out.'

'I can cancel the party,' said Graziana. 'It's not going to die a death without me. It's mostly Americans trying their darnedest to be Roman!'

'You *are* in a bad mood!' Harriet laughed. 'But please don't let me stop you if you really want to go. I can easily spend my time unpacking my toothbrush and thinking about tomorrow.'

'How well do you get on with Tarquin?' Graziana asked inquisitively.

'Well enough.' Harriet took up her suitcases to carry them into the adjoining room. 'He was—kindness itself on the island these past two days.'

'Which was strange, Tarquin doesn't go out of his way to be kind. He must have had a reason,' Graziana suggested.

'Perhaps he was sorry for me.'

'Sorry?' Graziana disappeared into the kitchen. 'He wouldn't put himself out just because he was sorry. He probably wanted to talk to Grandmother about Emmy.'

'It's—not our business.'

'I guess not.' Graziana flourished a saucepan. 'Will you have your eggs poached or scrambled, or shall I do a spectacular *risotto* with the left-overs?'

'The *risotto* will do nicely.'

'You're nothing if not original! How long are you going to stay in Rome?'

'As long as the Contessa needs me.'

'Aha!' said Graziana knowingly. 'That may be long enough.'

'I wish you wouldn't talk in riddles!'

'It's no riddle. I think my artful grandparent had more than one reason for asking you to come to Rome.'

'Such as?' Harriet put her suitcases down on the bedroom floor.

'I think you might be some sort of lure,' Graziana informed her from the kitchen.

'What an odd thing to say!' Harriet objected. 'I'm sure I don't look like bait, and I can't imagine what sort of fish your grandmother would like to catch.'

'I can,' Graziana said with passion. 'She's a scheming old —lady, if ever there was one, even though she does pretend to be above that sort of thing. She's always had her own way and always will. Grandfather spoiled her, of course, because he absolutely doted on her. *La Bella Renata!* The toast of Umbria in her heyday!'

The brittle, sophisticated American girl had suddenly become the passionate *signorina*, her flashing dark eyes glittering back at Harriet as she came to stand in the bedroom doorway.

'She's not going to rule my life!' she declared. 'Not all the time, and as for deciding whom I should marry she can forget it! I'll marry when I'm ready and whom I please.'

She was wholly determined to go her own way, and Harriet smothered a smile, thinking how like Tarquin she was in that moment and how much they both resembled their maternal grandparent.

In the end it was Harriet who cooked their frugal meal.

'I find it too difficult to talk and cook at the same time,' Graziana excused herself, 'and you do it all so well.' She carried her plate to a stool beside the electric fire. 'I think this is going to be fun,' she added, waving her fork in the direction of the bedroom. 'You and I together. We'll get on all right provided we don't tread on each other's toes too often. It ought to be easy,' she reflected. 'You cook and I learn to be tidy. Even Tarquin would agree with that.'

'He won't be here to witness your improvement after to-morrow,' Harriet pointed out regretfully.

'Cerano isn't all that far away,' Graziana reminded her, 'although he may not want us there too often.' She cleaned up the last of the rice, running her fork thoughtfully round the edge of her plate. 'I think he's wrong about Emmy, by the way. She's not the sort of person who would make him happy.'

'If he's in love with her you could be wrong.'

'Maybe. But Emmy was such a scatterbrain at one time. She had never any regard for money, as you know, and she liked to have all the beautiful young men in Rome dancing attendance on her. That's why I think Tarquin might be making a ghastly mistake.'

'Are they—engaged?'

'Heavens, no! It's much too soon, I guess, even for Emmy. I think she enjoys being a widow and having Tarquin to protect her.'

Deliberately Harriet guided the conversation into a less painful channel.

'What's been happening while I've been away?' she asked. 'Rome looks just the same.'

'It is, and how could it ever be different?' Graziana got

up to clear the plates. 'It's the Eternal City, isn't it, the same now as it was over two thousand years ago?'

'Except for the orgies!' Harriet laughed.

'I wonder! Surely you've heard of the jet set? But we're not exactly in that class, are we? At one time Emmy aspired to it, but Carlo hadn't enough money to gratify her whims. He was up to his eyes in debt when he drowned, but I expect you heard.'

'No.'

'Tarquin cleared it all up for Emmy's sake, I guess,' Graziana decided.

'She must be more than grateful to him.'

'Curiously enough, I believe she is.' Graziana went to the kitchen to make the coffee, which she did very well. 'I wouldn't like to be too sure, but I think she appreciates what Tarquin has done for her and would like to make amends.'

'By marrying him?' The words almost stuck in Harriet's throat.

'It wouldn't exactly quash the rumours, would it?' Graziana came back with the coffee. 'Some people take a fiendish delight in being able to say "I told you so" when the time comes.'

'I don't think we ought to talk about it,' Harriet said again.

'Do you want to go out?' Graziana asked, taking the hint. 'We could find some respectable *taverna* and drink coffee again, or a glass of wine while we watch the world go by.'

'Or we could walk,' Harriet suggested. 'It would help to digest the *risotto*!'

'You sure are a glutton for punishment,' Graziana reflected. 'I expect you walked all over Capri when you were there with Tarquin.'

But Harriet was determined not to be drawn into any further discussion about Tarquin.

'I'll get my coat,' she said. 'If I remember correctly Rome can be cold after dark.'

They walked for an hour through the busy streets, along the Via Sistina to the Piazza Barbarini and finally turning sharply into the Via dei Lucchesi until they found themselves standing before the Trevi fountain. The great cascade of water falling into its marble basin silenced them for a moment, and suddenly Harriet remembered how she had cast the traditional coin into the fountain more than a year ago in the hope that she would return to Rome. Well, she had returned, but it had not brought her happiness, so she would have no more to do with legend or superstition ever again.

'It's cold,' Graziana shivered. 'Let's go back.'

They retraced their steps, reaching the flat as a clock somewhere struck ten, and this time Harriet felt that she was made welcome.

'Stay as long as you like,' Grazianna invited without reserve.

CHAPTER THREE

IT was after ten the following morning before Harriet reached the shop, to find Tarquin already there. The streets had been crowded in the chaotic rush to work after the holiday, but she still apologised.

'I ought to have been here on time,' she said breathlessly, 'but I can make up for it tomorrow. You've been busy.'

She looked about her at the cluttered shop, at the show-cases piled high with silver and the area where the books were stacked. Tarquin had taken the silver out of the safe in the basement, to which he had the key, but the books were still in their packing-cases waiting to be catalogued.

'You've given yourself a gigantic task,' he observed. 'Sorting all this out is going to take days and an intelligent assistant.'

'I've got all the time I need,' Harriet assured him, taking off her coat to hang it in the cubbyhole in the office. 'The problem is to find the intelligent assistant.'

He hesitated.

'I'll find someone,' he promised, 'even if it is only to clean the silver.'

'What happened to Dino?' Harriet asked.

'I'm still searching for him. He was given a month's holiday in lieu of notice and we must hope he is still available.'

'He was the best parcel-tier I've ever seen.' She busied herself among the books which were her great delight. 'Do we open as soon as we have something on the shelves?'

'I think we should wait till tomorrow,' he decided. ' "Rome wasn't built in a day", etc!'

'What's that to do with it?'

'It's my invariable excuse for not rushing things!'

He was easier to get on with in the atmosphere of the

51

shop, Harriet thought, more relaxed, but no doubt that was because he would soon be returning to Cerano—and Emmy.

'How often do you come to Rome?' she asked.

'Not very often. Growing vines is a country occupation, although I do have to come from time to time.'

She wondered if one day he would bring Emmy to the shop. Where was Emmy? Graziana had said that she was at Cerano, but that might not be true. She took up a pile of books which was much too heavy for her.

'I'll stack these in the office and go through them when we've finished with the silver,' she said.

'Give them to me. They're far too heavy for you,' he declared.

'Tarquin, I'm used to this sort of thing!' she protested. 'I've worked with books all my adult life.'

In spite of her protest he took the stack of books from her.

'I can't let you take the risk of breaking a leg or falling up a ladder,' he said lightly. 'Your job should be purely managerial.'

'It will be once we've got all this sorted out.' She followed him to the bookshelves. 'I suppose this was my true reason for coming to Rome in the first place,' she mused. 'I've always wanted to work with rare editions.'

'And the silver?' he asked.

'That's fascinating, too. Your grandmother taught me all I know about it.'

'And now she's reaping her reward, I suppose.'

They worked for an hour and then he said it was time for some coffee.

'There's a *taverna* not too far away,' he reminded her. 'A very good one. You probably know it.'

'We always took our coffee in the office, but this will be a special treat.' She caught up her coat to follow him. 'I'll buy in some stores tomorrow from the *magazzino*.'

But tomorrow he would be gone! She tried to picture him on the family estate, finding it easy enough to conjure up a vision of him cantering up a mountain road, riding like a nobleman on a good horse, his silk shirt open at the neck, his eyes steadily on the way ahead. She knew that the estate was vast, with many acres of vineyards lying open to the sun on the slopes of a mountain, although she had never been there. Angelo had often spoken about it, even when his interests seemed to be elsewhere.

'Have you any news of Angelo?' she asked when they were seated in one of the secluded little booths in the *taverna*. 'It seems a long time for him to stay away from Rome.'

He remained silent while their coffee was brought to them by the *cameriere* who had taken their order.

'Harriet,' he said with a note of apology in his voice, 'I thought Angelo would have returned with you. We were under the impression that you had gone off together—it seemed too much of a coincidence at the time.'

An angry colour rushed into her cheeks.

'You could have given us the benefit of the doubt!' she suggested.

'I suppose so. You have my humble apologies.'

Was that all? The fact that she might have gone off with his brother was apparently nothing but a vague irritation to him, a small stain on the family name, but nothing more.

'Angelo and I were friends,' she said defensively. 'Playmates might be a better word.'

'He was fond of you.' If she hadn't known better she might have thought that there was accusation in his stern voice. 'Naturally we thought——'

'I told the Contessa why I was going back to London.'

'Because your mother was sick? Yes, she said that was your reason.'

It hadn't been her only reason, but how could she tell him that the scene on the cliff at Amalfi when he had held Emmy tenderly in his arms had crystallised her determination to go before it was too late and she had fallen hopelessly in love with him? I ran away, she thought, but what else was there to do? It had taken a year to consolidate the truth in her own mind, to bring her face to face with the realisation that she had been in love with Tarquin all along and was more deeply committed now than ever. She would love him all her life and he would never know.

Hastily she gulped down the hot, milky coffee, refusing the sticky cake the *cameriere* offered from a trolley.

'We must get back,' she decided hastily. 'There's far too much to do to spend our time gossiping!'

'Was that what we were doing?' Tarquin asked dryly. 'I'm sorry you ran away when you did, Harriet, but there's nothing we can do about it now.'

Not now that Emmy was free and he was going to marry her!

They walked the short distance to the shop in silence, working for the remainder of the day as if their lives depended on it, and by five o'clock there was a tidy assortment of polished silver in the showcases and most of the books were on the shelves.

Graziana wandered in to check on their progress.

'You've achieved wonders, but do I detect a certain sign of strain?' she remarked with a casual glance in Harriet's direction.

'Harriet is bound to be tired,' Tarquin said. 'She's been hard at it since early morning. I'll take you both out to dinner,' he offered unexpectedly.

'I can't go,' Graziana sighed regretfully. 'I have a heavy date with a fellow-American in Rome for the Culture. I must have promised to do a theatre with him in one of my weaker moments, but I know he won't understand a word.'

Tarquin looked round at Harriet.

'How about you?' he asked. 'Will you come?'

She shook her head.

'My idea of bliss at the present moment is a hot bath and supper in my dressing-gown,' she lied.

'Let me drive you back, in that case.'

He had expressed neither regret nor disappointment at her refusal, and surely that was the answer to their conversation in the *taverna*. She was no more to him than his

grandmother's assistant, someone who had stepped oblig-
ingly into the breach when the old lady was in need of
help. For that he would be grateful, but not disappointed
when she refused to have a meal with him.

It took less than ten minutes to reach the flat.

'Will you come in for a drink?' Graziana asked. 'There's
time.'

'Not tonight, thank you. I have an early start in the
morning.' He held out his hand to bid them goodbye. 'Good
luck with the business, Harriet.'

'I'll probably need it! Thanks for your help,' she said.

Graziana paused at the bedroom door.

'What happened?' she asked.

'Nothing—nothing at all!'

'When I came to the shop you both looked as if the Last
Trump had sounded.'

'You're being ridiculous!' Harriet returned sharply. 'I've
confessed to being tired.'

'Would you come out with me—and Jim—if I asked?'

'No.'

Graziana sighed.

'I have tried,' she pointed out.

'How far is it to Cerano?' Harriet asked, thinking of
Tarquin's early-morning start.

'Not very far. About two hours. Tarquin will make it by
mid-morning, I should think.' Graziana was watching her
closely. 'I do believe you're concerned about him!'

'I was curious—nothing more.'

'So long as you're sure.' Graziana gazed at her reflection
in the mirror. 'I suppose I shall have to shower before I go
out. I'm up to the eyes in paint. We had a blue session this
afternoon, hence the interesting shadows under my eyes.
Pity it will all wash off!'

'Would you like me to wait up for you?' Harriet asked.

'It won't be necessary. I have no intention of bringing
Jim back to my humble abode. We'll probably have supper
out somewhere after the show. Somewhere grand, I expect.
He tells me his father is an oil tycoon.'

'Mercenary!'

'Of course I am. Why not? My time is extremely valuable and Jim is a bore!'

'Graziana,' Harriet laughed, 'I don't think you mean a word of what you say!'

'Sleep on it and you might think differently in the morning!'

Harriet slept soundly enough in the single bed in the spare room jutting out on to the tiles where she could see the tops of the trees in the Villa Borghese steeped in moonlight and hear the sound of the early-morning bells pealing in the bright sunshine when she woke.

Something vaguely disturbing nagged at the back of her mind as she dressed, and when she finally picked up her handbag to go out she knew what it was. Tarquin had forgotten to give her the keys to the shop. He had locked up, putting them in his pocket automatically as they left.

What was she to do now? Graziana, who had evidently come in late, was still asleep.

There was a knock at the outside door and she ran to open it with her heart beating fast and fresh colour in her cheeks. It could not be anyone but Tarquin, delivering the missing keys. She opened the door and her heart sank.

'Dino!' she said. 'Where have you come from?'

The little Italian standing outside in the hallway gave her a dazzling smile.

'I come to deliver these.' He held up the missing keys. 'The young master gave them to me when he found me at my address last evening. He could not wait to deliver them to you this morning himself because he was in much of a hurry to be gone.'

'Thank you, Dino.' Harriet caught her lip between her teeth, fighting down her disappointment. 'Will you be coming back to work for the Contessa?'

He nodded eagerly.

'At once, *signorina*. We will perhaps go to the shop together now? It is not far to walk.'

They opened the shop as the first potential customers

began to throng the pavements. It was easy enough to spot the native product among the throng of visitors, Harriet thought, admiring the elegant grace of the Romans as they picked their way through the crowd. Suavely sophisticated and beautifully tailored, the men strolled in twos and threes or stood at the door of a coffee house in small groups to pass the time of day before they returned to their offices to begin work. Exigency seemed far from their minds as they walked leisurely in the Roman sunshine, and some of them stopped to admire the array of goods which Harriet had set in the window.

Bait, she thought, remembering her conversation with Graziana the day before, but quite a different sort of lure. Here was the rare and beautiful set out honestly for all to see, while Graziana had hinted at some dark and subtle reason for her return to Rome.

Of course, Graziana was exaggerating, or even just imagining a situation which did not exist. She tended to be dramatic when she was not pretending to be prosaic and completely down-to-earth.

Although many people stopped to gaze into the window it was mid-morning before they made their first sale, and it was little better during the next few days. Harriet, still busy cataloguing the piles of books at the back of the shop, began to despair, wondering if the Contessa and her delicate wares had been forgotten in so short a time. Dino, however, was eternally optimistic, advising her to cultivate patience and wait for the full tide of enthusiasm to flow their way once more.

'They will come,' he declared. 'It is always so when you have something of genuine worth to offer.'

For the first time Harriet was wearing the cameo necklace which Tarquin had given her on their way to Sorrento and Dino's connoisseur's eye had noticed it immediately.

'It is something of true value,' he said, admiring it again, 'and it is beautifully made. Perhaps it was given to you by a relative?'

A wave of strong colour dyed Harriet's cheeks.

'No—a friend,' she said. Her fingers fastened round the delicate gold chain. 'It was given to me in appreciation of a debt.'

'A great debt, surely,' the little Italian said. 'You must treasure it carefully, *signorina*. It would not do to lose it. Ah!' He turned to look through the glass door. 'We have now another customer. The news has got around!'

The man who came in through the doorway was tall and elegantly dressed, with the shrewd expression which stamped him immediately in their minds as a dealer. He approached the showcase where Harriet was replacing a silver cockerel, handing over his card.

'Can I help you?' she asked, looking up into the dark eyes with a smile. 'I don't think we have met before.'

'I deal mostly with the Contessa.' He bowed over her hand. 'But I hear that she is ill.'

'She will soon be well enough to return,' Harriet told him. 'At present she is convalescing on Capri.'

'Ah, blessed isle!' he smiled. 'I wish I had the time to go there more often, but that is not possible nowadays when everyone has to work.'

The title and coronet on the card he had proffered had not escaped Harriet's attention. He was a nobleman of some repute in the trade and she thought he had come to sell. She was wrong, however.

'I am here to collect two vases which the Contessa offered me some time ago,' he explained. 'I asked her to keep them for me because I was going abroad.'

Her employer hadn't mentioned the vases and Harriet supposed she had forgotten all about them.

'They must be here somewhere,' she reflected, preparing to search.

'Oh, no, I believe they are at the family home somewhere in the country,' her customer suggested. 'The Contessa thought it safer to keep them there than bring them to Rome before I needed them. I am buying for a museum, by the way.' He glanced at his watch. 'How long would it take you to get them for me?'

She could phone Tarquin immediately, Harriet thought, asking him to bring the vases to Rome, or her customer might wish to collect them in person.

He shook his head when she suggested the second course, again glancing at his watch.

'I have to catch a train for Florence in an hour,' he explained. 'Perhaps you would be kind enough to have the vases ready for me on my return in two days' time?'

'I'll do my best,' Harriet promised, making a rapid mental calculation as he prepared to leave. 'It gives me the week-end to get them. Yes, I should be able to do that.'

He thanked her and went away.

'I must phone Cerano,' she told Dino who had been listening from a discreet distance as he dusted the shelves. 'Do we have a telephone number in case of emergency?'

'For the Villa Elena?' Dino rummaged in an antique desk. 'It is here, to be sure, but I should be able to remember it. My memory is not what it was, alas!' he sighed, turning over the accumulation of papers which Harriet had been sorting out—bills and catalogues and letters of commendation from satisfied customers and the inevitable odd complaint. 'There's nothing here.'

'Perhaps we had better look elsewhere,' Harriet suggested, 'or consult the directory.'

'Ah, I have it at last!' Dino held up some headed writing-paper. 'I knew it was here all the time.'

They phoned the number several times to no avail, but at five o'clock they received what appeared to be a reluctant response. Dino had dialled the number and promptly he was in earnest conversation with the person at the far end of the line. He spoke in rapid Italian, tossing in the odd colloquial phrase which left Harriet far behind, but he seemed pleased with his efforts when he finally put down the receiver.

'There is no one at the villa at the present moment,' he explained. 'Everyone has gone away, but they will be returned tomorrow. That was my cousin Enrico speaking. He looks after the villa for the Contessa, but I could not ask him about the vases, for he would not know.'

'We must have them for Monday morning,' Harriet

frowned. 'Have you any suggestions, Dino?'

'Only that it would save time if you went to the villa personally tomorrow. It would be a nice change,' he said, 'and good for you to get into the country in such lovely weather if you have nowhere else to go.'

She had nowhere else to go, but the thought of descending on Tarquin uninvited kept her silent. He had seemed determined to protect his privacy on the family estate against all comers and no doubt he would take her visit as an invasion of that securely-guarded isolation and in the worst possible taste.

Yet this was business, and rather than lose the Contessa a valuable sale, she decided to go. It would save Tarquin the journey to Rome which he would have to make since there was no time to send the vases by post.

'I'll come with you,' Graziana offered unexpectedly when she explained her dilemma. 'Rome is completely dead at the week-end, except for the tourists.'

Harriet felt relieved. At least Graziana had a right to go to the Villa Elena, which was her grandmother's home.

The ancient Bugatti took the eastern way out of Rome in its stride at first, but after Tivoli with its spectacular fountains, the road began to climb steadily into the foothills of the Abruzzi and the little car began to show signs of age, as Tarquin had predicted, slowing their progress. Little walled towns appeared on every hilltop, most of them crowned by a spectacular castle or the ruins of one, standing out against the incredible blue of the sky as they made their slow progress towards Cerano. The snow of winter still lay white on the distant Apennines to the north, but they took a road going south again before they reached the outskirts of the estate. Surrounded by mountains, it lay in a sun-filled valley entirely given over to the cultivation of vines, and it was here that the de Filippos had produced the fine white wine which had made their name famous on two continents.

The vast area of terraced land sloping down to the valley floor took Harriet completely by surprise. It was like a small kingdom, surrounded by its guardian hills, a place where a man would become the overlord of all he could see. A fitting setting for Tarquin, she thought, catching her breath as she looked.

Graziana guided the car down a winding road through an orchard, finally pulling up at the door of a typically Renaissance villa set like a gem at the very heart of the estate. Tall cypresses stood in sentinel rows on either side of it, with a glimpse of other trees in the distance, and a gleaming fountain played in its marble basin in front. The fine doorway was reached by a branching stone stairway and was flanked on either side by marble columns and creeper-covered pergolas to afford shade on the warmest days.

Although it was not yet the siesta hour the villa seemed to be fast asleep. There was no movement anywhere in spite of the fact that the Bugatti had made a great deal of noise as it approached.

'We've drawn a blank,' Harriet observed. 'There doesn't seem to be anyone here at all.'

Graziana got out of the car, saying impatiently:

'There must be someone about, even if it's only an estate worker.'

'We can't do very much without Tarquin,' Harriet pointed out, wishing that they had not come.

'True,' said Graziana, turning into the orange grove which sheltered the loggia on one side. 'We'll see what we can find at the back.'

The rear of the villa appeared to be as deserted as the front, but when Graziana tried a side door it gave readily to her hand.

'All is not lost!' she exclaimed. 'Follow me, Harri, and perhaps we'll even be able to make ourselves a cup of tea.'

Harriet hung back.

'I don't think we should prowl around,' she objected, 'especially as Tarquin doesn't know we're here.'

Graziana turned towards her with a show of impatience.

'It's my grandmother's home,' she said. 'I have as much right to "prowl" as Tarquin.'

'All the same, we haven't been asked, and Tarquin *is* living here at present.'

'He'll always live here,' Graziana shrugged. 'It is his inheritance, but that does not mean to say that I can't visit whenever I like. Do be sensible, Harri, and stop worrying about what Tarquin might think!'

They went through a dim passageway into a small side hall and on into an enormous kitchen with a huge stone fireplace let into the wall and gleaming copper cooking utensils hanging on the chimney-breast. Enormous wooden cupboards with glass doors housed regiments of earthenware pots and jugs, while a dazzling array of lustre bowls and plates took pride of place on the high shelves above. A solid wooden refectory table stood in the middle of the scrubbed floor, its surface white and hollowed by years of constant use, and on it lay the remains of a frugal meal.

'Enrico!' Graziana yelled at the top of her voice. 'He must have been here a few minutes ago,' she turned to say to Harriet. 'It could have taken him all that time to go to the front door.'

As if to substantiate her suggestion the sound of shambling footsteps reached them from an inner passageway.

'Enrico!' Graziana shouted again. 'We're here, in the kitchen. You have no need to open the big door.'

Enrico had already opened it, however, and a blaze of sun greeted them as they reached the main hall. Furniture shrouded in dust-sheets stood all round the mosaic floor, proclaiming the fact that the house was no longer occupied to its fullest extent. Enrico, who was old and arthritic, hobbled into view, peering at them in the revealing light which streamed in through the open doorway.

'*Signorina*,' he said, 'I did not know it was you. I will open up the small *sala* immediately and bring some wine.'

He was delighted to see Graziana, who was an obvious favourite with him.

'He must be very old,' commented Harriet, watching as he hobbled off in the direction of the kitchen. 'Shouldn't we offer to help?'

'He'd be humiliated,' Graziana said. 'He'll bring wine and some of the little cakes his daughter bakes for visitors and he'll be in a seventh heaven of delight while he does it! He's about ninety, I think, but apart from the arthritis he's very fit. He would be greatly insulted if we thought he needed our help to do what he feels is his duty.' She walked quickly across the hall, flinging open the double doors which led into the little *sala*. 'We'll have to open the shutters. It's quite dark in here,' she said.

When the sun streamed in the room came immediately to life. It was quite small, leading out to a garden court where a little bronze satyr stood endlessly in the centre of a silent fountain. He looked so forlorn standing there alone, waiting for the water to flow, and yet there was a certain audacity about the tilted head crowned with budding horns and the goat-like ears which Harriet found almost repulsive.

'We used to tell Angelo he'd grow up like that!' her companion laughed, viewing the statuette through the glass doors which shut him out. 'But he never did believe us. The fountain was always in play when I came here in the old days as a child,' she mused. 'We were so young and able to telescope the past into the present without difficulty. Angelo used to tweak the satyr's tail and wish for everything he knew he shouldn't have!'

'And you?' Harriet asked. 'What did you hope for, Graziana?'

A strange expression crossed the younger girl's face.

'I won't tell you that,' she declared, half laughing, half serious. 'Because if I do, it may never happen.'

So Graziana's wish remained unfulfilled even now, Harriet thought uneasily, because she had seen a hint of pain in her companion's eyes.

When Enrico shuffled back with a tray bearing two crystal glasses and a bottle of wine he said that Tarquin was 'somewhere about'. He did not know where, but he thought that he might have gone to the Villa Coralo, as he generally did at this time of day.

Graziana looked upset.

'Maybe we can find the vases for ourselves,' she suggested, looking round the *sala*. 'They're sure to be here somewhere.'

'We can't just *take* them,' Harriet objected. 'We must find Tarquin and ask his permission.'

'I guess,' Graziana conceded, 'but it's quite a way to walk to the villa along a poor road. The Bugatti would never make it in its present exhausted condition. The villa was the old dower house and it's right on the edge of the estate.' She hesitated. 'Are you sure you want to go all that way?'

'The walk will do us good,' Harriet decided. 'We've been sitting in the car most of the morning.'

Graziana poured the wine in a reflective silence as Enrico returned with a platter of little rice cakes which his daughter had made, so obviously Tarquin ate at the Villa Ilena whatever else he did at the dower house.

'It's our own brew,' Graziana explained, holding up her glass to the light. 'What do you think of it?'

The wine looked like bottled sunshine as Harriet raised her glass, and she was suddenly reminded of the wine they had drunk at Anacapri which Tarquin had poured. It looked, and probably was, the same.

'I'm no connoisseur, of course, but it tastes delicious,' she said quietly.

'The "nectar of the gods"!' Graziana smiled. 'The wine of supreme happiness and love!'

'You've become quite romantic of a sudden!' Harriet selected a cake. 'Have you ever known "supreme happiness", Graz?'

'Well——' Her companion hesitated. 'Once or twice, perhaps, and I think we all know it when we're very young or first in love.'

'You sound as if it wasn't meant to last.'

'Occasionally it does.' Graziana finished her wine. 'I

guess my grandmother is still in love with the memory of her husband. She never remarried after he died, you see, and she speaks about him quite often.'

'A lifelong love,' Harriet murmured.

'You could say that, and I don't think I have the wrong facts. She was attractive enough to have married for a second time, but she never did.' Graziana opened the glass doors which led into the little courtyard. 'Let's go,' she said, 'now that we're full of good wine and good intentions.'

Evidently in a reminiscent mood, she tweaked the little satyr's tail as she passed, leading the way into the orange grove.

'I suppose Enrico will lock up behind us,' said Harriet, looking back at the open doors.

'All in good time, but he'll leave the *sala* as it is in case we come back,' Graziana declared. 'They can't use it very much when Tarquin is here alone. He works very hard and I guess he doesn't go in for entertaining, even on a modest scale.'

They walked rapidly along a gravelled drive and out on to the estate road where the woods came down on either side, thick and green in new leaf and providing a welcome shade from the midday sun. Beyond, the hillsides were clothed in new vines, terrace after terrace of them marching off as far as the eye could see on either side of the lovely valley which was Tarquin's secret domain. Harriet could imagine him riding there in splendid isolation, happily content in his role of master and determined to make a success of the task he had undertaken in his grandmother's name.

Presently they came to a small clearing where the ruins of an ancient chapel stood in the dappled sunlight, mute evidence of the distant past when the Christian monks had to worship in secret far away from pagan Rome. The woods had taken the ruins to themselves and made them beautiful, preserving all the quiet of the ages in that one small place, and Harriet could almost hear the silenced chapel bell ringing out from the ancient ivied tower.

'We're almost there,' said Graziana when they had left

the clearing behind. 'Not much further to walk now.'

The trees thinned out, giving pride of place to an olive grove, and presently they could see the pink-washed walls of the Villa Coralo ahead of them. It was a small house compared with the magnificent family villa they had just left, but it had the added charm of all small places because it had an intimate, lived-in look, standing on its terrace covered with flowers, and all the doors on one side open to the sun. A Greek bas-relief high on the wall above the door caught the light as they approached, and a tiny lizard slid away from the terrace steps to hide among the vines. Graziana hesitated.

'We'd better ring the bell,' she said.

Normally she would have gone in by the open terrace door, assured of her welcome, but she waited to ring the bell a second time.

'Tarquin may not be here, after all,' she said doubtfully.

Harriet drew in a deep breath.

'Someone must be in,' she said. 'All the windows are open.'

Before Graziana pulled the bell for the third time they heard footsteps approaching the heavy door from the inside, light steps crossing a mosaic floor to answer their summons at last.

Graziana stepped back as the door swung open and Harriet felt as if her heart had missed a beat. Not Tarquin but Emmy Luciano stood in the doorway, smiling her surprise at her unexpected visitors.

'Graz! And Harriet!' she cried. 'Please come in.'

Carlo Luciano's widow was a lovely girl to look at, fair as Titian's Flora, her profile pure Greek, her eyes as blue as the blue Tyrrhenian sea, and there seemed to be nothing forced about her welcome as she led them across the cool hall to the sunny little *sala* whose open windows led directly into the loggia they had seen from the front of the house.

'It is a great surprise,' she said in her heavily-accented English. 'Have you walked here from the villa, and have you seen Tarquin?'

'Not yet,' Graziana told her. 'But that's why we're here. We've come for some vases he has for one of the Contessa's customers and they're probably at the villa, but we couldn't take them without letting him know. Enrico said he would most likely be here,' she added, frowning.

'I am expecting him,' Emmy agreed, 'but not till later. Tarquin, he is a demon for work,' she laughed. 'Always he is riding through the estate, supervising and helping where he can, but today he has gone to Florence. He is not happy when he has nothing to do, but sometimes I think he works too hard. Yes, it is so,' she added, her blue eyes clouding. 'So many things have changed since a year ago,' she added. 'You, Harriet—you have gone back to your own country, but now you are returned. Will you stay in Rome, do you think?'

It seemed to Harriet that she had to bring herself back from a great distance to answer the simple question.

'For the present,' she heard herself saying as she looked into the other girl's amazingly blue eyes. 'I'm managing the shop again.'

'Tarquin has told me, and he is glad because of his grandmother.' Emmy turned to ring the bell beside the chimneypiece. 'You will take some wine?' she asked. 'You must be hot and weary after so long a walk in the sun.'

The manner in which she gave her order to the servant who answered her summons turned Harriet's blood to ice. Emmy was so lovely, so assured, living here in the dower house as she had once lived at Amalfi, the beautiful custodian of a lovely bijou home, and it seemed only too obvious that Tarquin had brought Carlo's widow to be near him until he was able to marry her.

Shocked, Harriet wanted to turn away, but Emmy confronted them with gracious ease.

'Perhaps I can give you tea if you have already had some wine,' she suggested, leading the way on to the sunlit terrace. 'I make it to please Tarquin, in the English manner, for his father was an Englishman, was he not? Perhaps he will come early if Enrico has told him of your visit,' she added thoughtfully. 'I hope so, because it is a long walk back through the estate. I have no car at present to offer to take you. I do not go often to Rome.'

She seemed far removed from the flighty socialite Harriet remembered. Parties and fashionable clothes had once been Emmy Luciano's main interest in life as she had sought to be the most popular hostess in Rome, but now it all seemed to have turned sour on her. She looked more subdued and content to be here, waiting in her lonely retreat for Tarquin's return.

Graziana moved to the edge of the terrace to look out over the garden where orange and lemon trees grew in great profusion. She seemed to be puzzled by Emmy's manner, not quite knowing what to say to her.

'We really ought to return to the villa,' she protested as their hostess rejected the wine and ordered tea. 'We may meet Tarquin on the way.'

'You must stay now that you have come,' Emmy said. 'I have so few visitors,' she added on a note of sadness which stressed her isolation from her former world of entertaining and laughter. 'Sometimes I think that the days will never end.'

'You have Tarquin,' Garziana reminded her unkindly.

'Ah! Tarquin,' Emmy smiled. 'What would I do without him? He is so kind, so *tenero*. I can never sufficiently thank him for all he has done for me, and I so little worthy of tenderness!'

She set out the fine china cups on the tray, her slim hands not quite steady as she poured their tea.

'You like it strong?' she asked, turning her sad blue eyes on Harriet. 'With milk and sugar?'

'Please.'

Harriet could not look back at her with anything but pity, for it was obvious that Emmy had gone through a traumatic experience when her husband died which had touched her deeply. She was no longer the irresponsible girl who had laughed and played in the Amalfi sunshine and kept men dangling on a hook for the fun of it; she was no

longer the child-wife who had spent money recklessly for
her own adornment, kicking over the traces of convention-
ality wherever she went. This Emmy was different, and
even Graziana seemed to be aware of the subtle change in
her.

When they were half way through the meal they heard
the sound of horse's hoofs coming along the short drive
from the road and presently Tarquin appeared at the end of
the terrace, a tall, commanding figure seated on a black
horse with his hat pulled well down over his eyes to protect
them from the sun.

'I heard you were here,' he said, dismounting in front of
them. 'I have been in Florence.' His gaze remained steadily
on Harriet's flushed face. 'Has anything happened to worry
you?'

He came across the terrace to where they were seated,
pausing momentarily to lay a reassuring hand on Emmy's
shoulder in a gesture of protectiveness which seemed completely natural to him.

'No.' Harriet had to moisten her lips before she could go
on. 'Do you remember the Contessa putting some vases
aside for a customer?' she asked. 'Well, he turned up to
collect them yesterday, but he couldn't spare the time to
come all his way and we couldn't reach you on the phone.
The villa seemed to be shut up.'

Suddenly appalled, she realised what she was implying,
but he did not even look in Emmy's direction.

'Enrico is very deaf,' he said. 'If he was out in the garden,
as he usually is, he wouldn't hear the phone and I have been
working late since my return. We have big shipments of
wine going out in a few days' time and there is much to do.
The vases,' he went on. 'Yes, I know about them. They
have been quite safe at the villa, I assure you.'

'We'll take them back with us,' Graziana offered. 'Harri
thought it would save you coming all the way to Rome
with them.'

'That was thoughtful of Harriet,' Tarquin said almost
dryly. 'As it happens, I am grateful.' He accepted a cup of

tea from Emmy but refused a cake. 'Time is precious to me just now.'

Harriet found herself forced to meet his demanding gaze. He looked quite ruthless, his grey eyes fully upon her as he raised the delicate cup to his lips. Was he trying to pretend that his relationship with Emmy meant nothing? she wondered. But no; Tarquin would never pretend!

When he had finished his tea he rose to his feet.

'Thank you, Emmy,' he said. 'I will see you tomorrow.'

They exchanged an understanding glance as Emmy rose to see them to the door.

'If you walk a little way I'll bring the car to meet you,' Tarquin promised as he vaulted into the saddle. 'It's about the worst time of day to be walking in the sun.'

With a quick tightening of the rein he pulled his horse's head round, galloping off through the trees.

'Perhaps you will come again, Harriet,' Emmy said. 'When you are not so busy at the shop.'

'We're right at the beginning of the season,' Harriet tried hard not to sound brusque. 'But if you're in Rome——'

Emmy smiled.

'When I am in Rome I have so much to do,' she said, 'but I will try to visit you. Do not expect a customer, though,' she added lightly, 'for I have very little money now.'

'Something has happened,' said Graziana as they walked away. 'She's quite changed.'

'I couldn't pass an honest opinion,' Harriet answered. 'I only met her once or twice and we didn't seem to have much in common.'

'Can you imagine Tarquin being in love with her?' Graziana asked dramatically.

'I—don't know. If she's changed so much they could be in love, and he has brought her to live on the estate,' Harriet pointed out unhappily.

'H'mm!' Graziana plucked at a nearby mandarin bush. 'I guess I can't figure that one out. Tarquin rarely does anything without consulting Grandmother.'

'She would object, of course.'

'I guess. Well, not to worry too much! Tarquin will work things out in his own way,' Graziana decided.

They walked in the soft light under the olive trees, thinking their separate thoughts until they heard a car coming towards them and Tarquin pulled up at the edge of the grove.

'Get in,' he said. 'I have to go round by the lodges to make sure that everything is in top gear for tomorrow. It won't take more than half an hour.'

They were interrupting his work routine, but Harriet was glad to be able to relax a little before they again reached the Villa Elena. It would be interesting to see the wine being bottled and the preparations for the shipment of mature wine which he had already mentioned.

The big bottling sheds were a hive of industry and the sweet aroma of wine pervaded everything, reminding her of the scent of orange flowers and bergamot as they passed slowly between the long trestles where the bottles stood ready to be packed. Sure hands filled the cases while other hands closed and stamped them to await transportation at the earliest opportunity. The sheds were comparatively modern, but beyond them lay the vast stone caverns where the vats rested, one above the other, in long, regimented rows, waiting for time to do his work. Dark-haired men with keen eyes and experienced palates moved between the rows, pulling off a tester here and there into small, long-handled cups which they tried and rejected or accepted as they went along. Tarquin spoke to some of them in rapid Italian, asking if all went well.

'*Si! Si, signorino!*' One of them made an ecstatic kissing movement with his hands. '*Bello! Bello vino!*'

They returned to the sunlight not far from the Villa Elena itself.

'We can walk from here,' said Tarquin. 'Luigi may need the car.'

Returning to the villa was an odd experience for Harriet. Now that she was here at Tarquin's invitation she could

look about her without feeling guilty of trespass and he
seemed quite willing to conduct her on a tour of his grandmother's home. In spite of the fact that most of the furniture was temporarily shrouded in dust sheets, each room
appeared as a treasure house of *objets d'art* accumulated
by the family over the years, and the lovely seventeenth-
century villa was a fitting setting for them all. Fine bronze
and delicate glass, marbles and striking bas-reliefs adorned
the walls in room after room, but it was the portraits which
held her entranced. Looking down at her from frame after
frame she saw a man on a thoroughbred horse, and all of
them with the strong features of the man by her side.

'Ancestors,' Tarquin said carelessly. 'We look shock-
ingly alike.'

'This one?' she asked, putting out her hand to touch the
ornate gilt frame.

'My maternal grandfather. That is why the Contessa is
so proud of me,' he laughed. 'It helps to cancel out my
English background!'

'You're amazingly alike,' she mused. 'It would be almost
impossible to tell the difference but for your eyes. Though,
perhaps——'

'You were going to say?' he queried, aware of her hesitation.

'He has a generous mouth,' she decided. 'Oh, I'm sorry!'
she apologised immediately. 'I had no right to say that.'

'A bit of honest criticism doesn't come amiss from time
to time.' He looked amused by her candid assessment of
him. 'Since you find me wanting in generosity I won't try to
convince you otherwise, but I thought I could be kind when
the need arose.'

'I'm sure you can.' She turned from the portrait of his
grandfather. 'You've proved it in the past.'

'What do you do in Rome when you are not working at
the shop?' he asked.

'I walk. There's still so much of old Rome for me to
see, and I want to visit Tivoli again for more than just an
hour.'

'You should have a car at your disposal,' he decided.

'Graziana has promised to take me to Tivoli.'

'In that dreadful buggy? I would advise you not to go if you value your life. I will send a car for you one of these days, or come myself,' he promised.

'You're very kind, Tarquin, but I do know how busy you are on the estate,' she acknowledged, although her heart was beating fast.

'One good turn deserves another, don't you think? It was thoughtful of you to come to collect the vases and save me the round trip to Rome.'

'I wasn't quite sure what to do,' she confessed, 'but it did seem a shame to lose a sale.'

'I'll pack them for you in the morning.' He moved towards the gallery door. 'You'll stay here overnight, of course, as my guest. There's no point in returning to Rome so late in the afternoon, and if the weather remains fine tomorrow I'll show you the rest of the estate.'

'Why not?' Graziana asked, coming towards them across the mosaic floor. 'It will please Grandmother to know that we visit with you occasionally.'

'If it won't really be any trouble,' Harriet said.

'No trouble at all,' he shrugged. 'Enrico and his daughter look after me very well and we are almost self-supporting on the estate. You will not starve.' He smiled in his cousin's direction.

'It might be fun,' Graziana suggested as he walked away. 'We could ride out to the lake during the morning, although I suppose I should go to Mass. I wonder if Tarquin brings Emmy up here when he has visitors,' she added thoughtfully.

Harriet, who had been thinking about Emmy, shook her head.

'He may find it more convenient to go to the Villa Coralo on his own.'

Tarquin gave his orders and their rooms were prepared for them, but Emmy did not make her appearance at the dinner table or even afterwards when they sat on the edge of the loggia sipping their coffee as if, indeed, they were a family gathered naturally at the close of a busy day.

The light appeared to linger above the olive grove longer than usual and the sweet smell of orange blossom filled the air, mingling with the heavy scent of mimosa and thyme. When the stars finally appeared in the darkening sky the whole world seemed to be at peace.

Suddenly a nightingale began to sing, filling the garden with glorious sound as it poured out its heart in the darkness in a burst of joy. The hidden songster, voice of the night, seemed more than Tarquin could bear. He rose abruptly, his hands thrust deep into the pockets of his white dinner jacket as he walked to the terrace edge.

'Time to go to bed,' Graziana suggested, stretching in her chair. 'I do believe I'm tired.'

Tarquin walked to the foot of the staircase with them, bidding them goodnight as the telephone bell shrilled across the hall.

'Goodnight,' Harriet said as he went to answer it.

CHAPTER FOUR

In the morning he had gone, leaving a message for them with Enrico to say that he had left early for Florence but hoped to be home again before nightfall.

'I wonder if Emmy has gone with him,' said Graziana as they lingered over their breakfast. 'We can always go and see.'

'No!' Harriet was adamant, her heartbeats like slow hammer-blows. 'We have no right to spy on them.'

Graziana laughed.

'Aren't you even the tiniest bit curious?' she asked.

'Not in the way you mean.' Harriet rose to her feet. 'If we sit here all morning I'll never see the estate.'

'We could ride,' Graziana suggested. 'I have a pair of old breeches in my room which may still fit, and you could borrow my jeans.'

'I'm not a very good horsewoman,' Harriet objected. 'In fact, I've only been on a horse once or twice in my life.'

'That wouldn't matter,' Graziana assured her. 'We'd only be jogging along between the olives most of the time. Take a chance,' she urged. 'I won't gallop off and leave you, I promise!'

The prospect of riding through the golden landscape was enchanting and Harriet gave in with a smile.

'Tarquin has a whole stable full of horses he can't possibly exercise,' Graziana explained as she searched her room for the jodhpurs she had laid aside some time ago. 'I guess you'd better wear them,' she decided when they were finally discovered in an old trunk. 'They look too tight for me now and, honestly, I prefer jeans.'

'You're quite sure?'

'I wouldn't say so if I didn't mean it.' Graziana pulled

a woollen jersey over her head. 'I haven't worn this for a long time, either, but it seems to fit.'

They set out for the stables where she harnessed two small palomino ponies for them to ride.

'I'm being magnanimous,' she grinned. 'I'd far rather ride Tarquin's stallion, but I guess he wouldn't be too keen on that!'

They rode out into the sunshine and through the olive grove where the light filtered between the leaves in dappled shade, and then they began to climb. Up and up they went, the delightful little ponies treading carefully between the vines until they came to the ultimate barrier of the hills where they could look down on a blue lake and all the estate lay spread out before them, like a map.

'There's the Villa,' said Graziana, pointing, 'and on the other side of the lake you can see the road with all the workers' houses dotted in between. The villa was built on Etruscan foundations, so there must have been an ancient city here at one time. I find it all very fascinating, although I wouldn't like to have lived so long ago.'

The wind in their faces was cool and sweet, tempering the hot sunshine, and Harriet gazed about her in delight. Away to the north she could see more mountains with the snow still white on their peaks, and she traced the course of a river running westward to the sea. Directly in front of her, looking down the valley, she could see the narrow road that led through the orange groves to the Villa Coralo.

'We'll go down that way,' Graziana decided, urging her pony to a trot. 'If she hasn't gone off with Tarquin we can ask Emmy to give us lunch.'

Following reluctantly in her wake, Harriet could not help wondering if they would find Emmy at the villa, but perhaps she went everywhere with Tarquin when she could. It would be perfectly natural if they were soon to marry, as Graziana supposed.

When they came nearer to the villa they could hear a dog barking.

'It's down by the lake,' Graziana said. 'We'll go that way.'

She urged her pony along a side track, making her way beneath the gnarled old fig trees which surrounded the lake while Harriet followed at a distance, half reluctant to go to the dower house a second time.

Before they reached it, however, they saw Emmy walking with a little dog on the far side of the lake, and even with the bright stretch of azure water between them she looked lonely and introspective as she made her way along the lakeshore. Even Graziana drew her pony to a halt, regarding her with a certain amount of pity.

'She looks so—dejected,' she reflected. 'So lost, but perhaps that's just my vivid imagination exercising itself in the wrong direction again. Do you think she might be regretting the past?'

'How could I possibly tell?' shrugged Harriet. 'I only met her once or twice and then it was in a crowd.'

'Like that last time at Amalfi before the accident?' Graziana was frowning. 'I wish I knew what had really happened.'

'There was a sudden storm,' Harriet said beneath her breath, reliving it all again. 'It was so dark and the sea was so wild all of a sudden it seemed to sweep the speed-boat away in a few seconds. I was in the other boat, following behind, but there was very little to be seen. It was only when we finally reached the shore that we realised they were in difficulty.'

'It's all a complete mystery, although the police tied it up as best they could. Another drowning accident among so many!' Graziana turned her pony's head in the direction of the Villa Coralo. 'It seems to have taught Emmy a lesson.'

'An expensive one,' Harriet agreed beneath her breath as Emmy looked up to recognise them with a wave of her hand.

The little dog ran to meet them, barking excitedly.

'I wondered if I would meet you,' said Emmy, lifting it into her arms. 'You must not bark, Sergio! These two ladies are my friends.'

Harriet dismounted to stroke the dog's silky coat and he licked her hand enthusiastically.

'You have been accepted,' Emmy informed her, smiling a little. 'Will you come to the villa and have something to eat with me? I would be glad of your company if you have the time to spare.'

'Graziana suggested it only a moment ago,' Harriet said, wondering why she should feel so quickly drawn to this new Emmy who bore hardly any resemblance to the Emmy she had once known. 'If you're sure we won't be a nuisance, I'd like to come.'

'I am often lonely,' Emmy confided, walking beside them, 'but I love this place and Tarquin has been so kind. There is nothing I need that he fails to provide, but perhaps you know him well enough to understand such thoughtfulness,' she added. 'He will go out of his way to help whenever he is asked.'

That was probably why she had been met at the airport and taken to Capri, Harriet thought. In helping his grandmother Tarquin was being kind.

Graziana left them to unsaddle the ponies.

'Let them loose in the pasture,' Emmy directed. 'They love to kick up their heels on the grass.'

So Tarquin's pale little palominos were no strangers to the Villa Coralo! Harriet followed Emmy into the cool shade of the loggia with the bitter little thought in her mind and a vision of Tarquin standing in the shadows smiling his enigmatic smile as Emmy rang the bell to order their lunch, which she had already helped to prepare.

It was a pleasant meal, the first course consisting of a shrimp dish which was new to Graziana.

'If it's easy to make you must let me have the recipe,' she said, passing her plate for a second helping. 'I'd no idea you were such a good cook, Emmy.'

'I wasn't until I came here,' Emmy admitted, 'and then it was necessary for me to learn. Tarquin likes this dish,' she added simply, 'and so we make it often, but it is really Gina who is the expert.'

The young Italian girl who had come in with the second course blushed shyly at the generous compliment. Typical of her country, she had the laughing eyes and broad hips of the peasant woman which she swung unconsciously as she walked.

'Crêpes Mona,' she announced, lifting the lid of the covered dish to allow a delicate aroma to escape. 'You will like —*si*?'

'I certainly will,' Graziana agreed, sniffing appreciatively. 'You've no idea how nice it is to have freshly cooked food for a change. Usually my meals come straight out of a packet.'

They sat for a long time, talking about Rome until Graziana decided that they must go:

'Tarquin will be home,' she said, 'and we really must get back to Rome.'

But Tarquin appeared even before they had re-saddled the ponies. They heard the sound of the car and the silence as it came to a halt at the terrace steps, and something about that silence kept them arrested where they stood. There seemed to be no sound anywhere in the garden as their eyes met.

'He's back early,' Graziana observed after a moment, 'but perhaps he meant to come here first, anyway.' She tightened a girth with a quick frown. 'I expect they want to be alone,' she said bluntly. 'Shall we go?'

'We can't go without saying goodbye to Emmy,' Harriet pointed out unhappily, 'but we can leave them together as quickly as possible afterwards.'

She took her rein from Graziana to walk back towards the villa. Half-way there she could see Tarquin on the terrace in earnest conversation with their hostess and it looked as if Emmy was fighting back tears. Finally she put her head down on Tarquin's shoulder, as if weeping, while he put an arm about her in a warm show of affection which turned Harriet's heart to ice.

'We can't go in—not yet,' she whispered to Graziana who had followed her. 'Emmy is terribly upset.'

'I guess so.' Graziana led her pony back along the path. 'But we can't wait for ever.'

They stood for a few minutes longer while the ponies cropped the grass under the trees, and then they went back to the loggia where Emmy was waiting alone.

'Tarquin has come,' she said. 'He brought me some things I needed. He has not had a very successful day in Florence, after all.'

A small, awkward silence followed in which Graziana got up on to her pony's back.

'Thanks for the crêpes Mona,' she said. 'I'll get the shrimp recipe some other time.'

They rode off before Tarquin could join them, taking the direct road to the Villa Ilena instead of the narrower paths among the vines. Tarquin drew up almost as soon as they had stabled the palominos.

'I'm glad you went to see Emmy,' he said. 'She is very lonely.'

'We thought you wouldn't mind us taking the ponies,' Graziana said, ignoring his reference to Emmy's loneliness. 'We went right to the top of the valley. It was sure beautiful. We saw Emmy by the lake when we were on our way back. Has she given up the Amalfi house?'

'Some time ago.' Tarquin was frowning. 'It was much too big and too expensive to maintain.'

Harriet said in a choked voice:

'We really ought to go if we're to get back to Rome before dark.'

He did not try to detain them.

'I've promised to have supper with Emmy after I've been over the estate,' he said.

His hurried visit to Florence had cancelled out his morning's inspection; otherwise he might have gone with them to the head of the valley, riding his sleek black horse to the manner born.

'I'll parcel up the vases while you change,' he said. 'I'm glad you enjoyed your ride.'

Behind the polite words Harriet sensed a deep frustration. His visit to Florence had not been successful and she could not help wondering why he had gone there at such short notice. He was not the sort of person to show disappointment easily, but the dark frown was still in evidence when he called her into the *sala* to hand over the vases she had come to collect.

'They're quite rare,' he explained. 'You will see that when you come to examine them and I don't know why my grandmother has decided to part with them. Perhaps she was persuaded, but I hardly think so!' He smiled at the suggestion. 'She is generally very sure of what she wants to do.' He turned to look at her. 'Could I ask you another favour, Harriet?' he said.

'Of course you can.' She had sounded much too eager. 'I—if there's anything I can do to help.'

He lifted a small bronze statuette of the god Cupid, an exquisite thing of delicate workmanship poised on a pillar of fluted marble.

'I want you to sell it,' he said. 'It should bring a good price if you can find the right buyer.'

She bit her lip, thinking how pathetic the little winged god of love looked as he stood there waiting to be valued by someone who no longer wanted him.

'Are you parting with family treasures?' she asked bluntly.

He looked down at her in quick surprise.

'I have no need to part with the family heirlooms,' he said coldly. 'This belongs to Emmy. I bought it for her some time ago in Venice, but now she wishes to part with it. It is nothing like as valuable as the vases, you understand, but it should bring a fair price.'

'I'll do what I can,' she promised. 'What would you consider "a fair price"?'

'I have no idea. You know the current market better than I do.'

She did not want to sell the little god, for Emmy or anyone else, and she could not understand Emmy wanting to part with it when it had been a gift from Tarquin. He had been almost casual about it, but surely he had been a little hurt by Emmy's decision to sell? It seemed, though, that she needed the money.

'Do your best,' said Tarquin, packing the little god of

love as carefully as he had parcelled the more precious vases. 'You should manage to sell it quite quickly. There are plenty of German tourists about with a lot of money in their pockets.'

'It's hardly the sort of thing the Germans go for.' Harriet picked up the little Cupid. 'They prefer the more solid pieces. A French or an American buyer would be more likely.'

'Not an Englishman?' he asked, smiling.

'I'd like it to go to England,' Harriet said.

'You are far too sentimental. After all, it is only a little bronze god.'

'The god of love,' she heard herself pointing out foolishly.

'Harriet, do you really believe in love?' he asked lightly.

'Why not?' She turned to face him, her gaze steady on his. 'It can hurt you—it can turn its head away when you're most involved, but you have to believe in it because it can also be tender and beautiful—and sometimes true.'

'Good for you, Harri!'

The voice, light and teasing as a summer's wind, came from the open terrace doors and they turned to find Angelo standing there, looking in at them. He was no different from what he had always been, slim and not very tall, with a pair of bright blue eyes which were constantly teasing and a mop of curling hair which lay on his forehead like burnished gold. The blue eyes continued to search their faces for a moment before the Contessa's younger grandson came into the room.

'Sorry if I'm breaking anything up,' he apologised, 'but I did phone to say I was coming, although Enrico does seem to be deafer than the proverbial post these days. I thought I'd got through to him because he chanted something about "letting you know". How are you, my dear brother?' he ran on. 'Pleased to see me, I hope.'

'More than pleased,' Tarquin assured him in a cool voice. 'Where have you been?'

'America. I should have written to you, but I knew that

I wouldn't stay there for any length of time. It was just not my scene.' He turned to Harriet. 'Long time no see,' he remarked. 'What have you been doing with yourself while I've been away, Harri? I hope you haven't married Tarquin?'

His smile was mischievous, his dancing blue eyes flashing in his brother's direction for a moment as he made his outrageous suggestion.

'I'm not married,' Harriet answered stiltedly, 'and I went back to England a year ago because my mother was ill.'

Tarquin's expression changed, the frown disappearing from his brow.

'You could have let us know,' he said to his brother. 'It has been a great strain on your grandmother, wondering where you were.'

'Surely she knew that no harm could come to her lamb?' Angelo laughed. 'What's a year, anyway, out of a lifetime?'

'It can mean a great deal when someone is as old as Grandmother, and as caring,' Tarquin pointed out.

His brother's smile vanished.

'You could be right,' he conceded more seriously, 'but she always believed in us trying our wings. Well!' He looked about him. 'Here I am! Do I stay, or do you feel that I might be surplus to your requirements on the estate now that you have taken over?'

'If you want to work,' Tarquin assured him, 'you are welcome to stay.'

'Thanks!' Angelo's tone was loaded with sarcasm. 'I'll see how it goes, but I think Rome will beckon me sooner or later.' He looked at Harriet.

'You must make your own decision, of course,' Tarquin answered, interpreting that look. 'No one will force you to work here against your will.'

They went out through the terrace door as Graziana returned from the stables.

'Angelo!' she exclaimed, her voice full of shocked surprise as she stood on the terrace steps staring up at them.

'In the flesh,' Anglo agreed. 'Don't look so flabbergasted,

my dear cousin, especially as I've come straight from the land of your birth and have much to tell you.'

'You've been to America?' Graziana gasped. 'When? For how long, for goodness' sakes?'

She had regained some of her composure, but the effort she had made was obvious. In that first moment of recognition her heart had been laid bare for anyone to see. Graziana had been in love with her cousin for a long time, although it did not seem as if Angelo appreciated the fact.

'For almost a year,' he said. 'I went to Paris first to— get away from everything.' He looked round at Tarquin, but his brother made no sign. 'The accident shook me,' he confessed. 'I had no idea anything like that could happen so quickly. Then I got a job and went to New York.'

'You could have written,' Graziana accused him.

'I recognise that now, but at the time I was very busy. You know—a new venture and all that sort of thing. I was up to the eyes in it and then, suddenly, it all folded. I feel now that I was some sort of stooge for these people. They needed me for a certain length of time and then—finish!'

'What were you doing?' Tarquin asked coldly.

'Photography. I thought I had it made, as a matter of fact.'

'You have always been keen enough,' Tarquin acknowledged, 'but perhaps you've got it out of your system this time.'

Angelo looked uncertain.

'Once an artist, always an artist,' he grinned. 'I could just try again.'

A flash of anger spread across Graziana's face.

'Isn't it about time you made up your mind what *exactly* you want to do with your life?' she demanded. 'You can't go on being a playboy for ever.'

Angelo flushed, his bright eyes suddenly dimmed.

'You make me sound like a *becero*, but I do not want to act like one,' he declared. 'Is it so shameful to want to turn over a new leaf?'

'If that's what you really mean to do,' Graziana said

quietly, 'no one will stand in your way, little angel, but why do you have to come and go as you please without considering anyone else?'

'If you mean Grandmama, I am sorry,' her cousin answered contritely enough. 'Perhaps I do care about some things,' he added. 'Perhaps I am now a reformed character and mean to stay.'

Again he looked in Harriet's direction and something in his expression caused a wave of hot colour to stain her cheeks. Graziana moved swiftly across the terrace.

'Are you going?' Angelo asked. 'I will drive you both back to Rome.'

'I have my own car,' Graziana told him stiffly. 'There's no need for you to rush back to Rome.'

'I was going, anyway,' Angelo assured her. 'What sort of buggy have you got?'

'A Bugatti,' his cousin answered with unconscious humour. 'It huffed and puffed a bit on the way out, but it will get us back, I guess.'

'I'll follow you,' said Angelo. 'The Bugatti I must see!'

Harriet hugged the parcel containing the little god of love close to her breast as she went down the terrace steps by Tarquin's side. Cupid, who had once ruled over gods and men and was now so powerless to help her as she turned to say goodbye to the only man she had ever loved.

'I'll let you know as soon as I've sold the statuette,' she promised. 'I'll get the best price I can for it.'

They drove direct to Rome, pulling up at the flat as the Angelus rang out over the quiet city. It was a day of bells ringing from every tower and campanile to fill the air with glorious sound.

Angelo drew up behind them a moment or two later.

'I hope you are going to invite me in,' he said. 'I have nowhere else to go.'

'We didn't get to do any shopping before we left,' Graziana informed him bluntly, 'but you're welcome to what we have.'

'We'll eat out,' he decided. 'I'm sure there's a "little place around the corner" that will accommodate us, or we could buy some wine and have fun with the left-overs if you'd rather.'

'We'll eat out,' Graziana said sharply. 'Where are you going to stay?'

Angelo hesitated.

'I was hoping you could offer me a couch or something,' he suggested after a moment.

'We have very little room.'

'I'm not very big.'

'Oh, all right!' Graziana agreed. 'You can sleep on the couch, but if you refuse to get up in the morning you'll be left to make your own breakfast.'

'I'll take the risk!' He seemed glad of the offer of accommodation, at least for the present. 'I expected to stay with Grandmama. I didn't know she had been ill.'

'We would have written to you if we'd known where to find you,' Graziana pointed out. 'Will you go to see her? She's at Anacapri in a rented villa, convalescing for a while.'

'I'll go as soon as I can.' He glanced in Harriet's direction. 'Would anyone like to come with me?'

'We're all much too busy,' Graziana told him, saving Harriet a reply.

She could not have returned to Capri after that perfect weekend, Harriet thought. Not with Angelo, who was never serious for more than a moment at a time.

He was excellent company, however, when it came to going out on the town. The restaurant he chose was not too fashionable, but it was busy and gay, the kind of place where Rome watched Rome go by, and they were ushered to a table by a smiling waiter who took Angelo's order with an elaborate bow. There was no doubt that her cousin was an amusing companion and very soon Graziana had ceased to frown as she countered his many quips, meeting them with her own. The restaurant was quite full, even at this early hour when the small band of musicians were just beginning to tune up, and Harriet looked about her with a new excitement in her eyes. She was determined to enjoy Rome in spite of everything.

In the morning she was first up and was making her breakfast in the tiny kitchen when Angelo came through from the living-room, tousle-headed and yawning, as if he had never been to sleep at all. He was wearing a pair of Graziana's pyjamas, which were far too small for him, and looked like a little boy lost.

'What they lack in length I gain in the width!' he grinned, gazing down at his half-mast state.

'I heard that!' Graziana yelled from the bathroom. 'Don't forget you're like a skeleton!'

'Are you going back to Cerano right away?' Harriet asked, measuring out three bowls of cereal.

'I could stay if you asked me nicely,' he decided.

She looked impatient.

'I won't be your excuse,' she declared. 'Besides, I have to work.'

'Curiosity prompts me to come to the shop.' He sat down at the kitchen table, pulling one of the bowls towards him.

'I'd be far too busy to entertain you,' Harriet told him.

'I could wrap your pretty ornaments when you have a sale,' he suggested, pouring far too much milk on his cereal.

'Dino does that very nicely, thank you.'

'You *are* in a bad mood this morning, Harri! What else are you giving me to eat?'

'I'm expecting you to make your own toast,' Harriet said firmly, 'and there's plenty of fruit.'

'You realise, of course, that you're being outrageously cruel?'

'I'm doing my best to be practical.'

'Why did you come back to Rome?' He dropped two pieces of bread into the electric toaster. 'Was it to try your luck with Tarquin?'

Caught unaware by the blunt question, she could not answer him immediately.

'I do believe it was!' he grinned. 'But you didn't bid

each other a fond farewell yesterday, as lovers do.'

'Leave it, Angelo!' Graziana had come to Harriet's rescue, appearing in the open doorway in her dressing-gown. 'You've got plenty to think about without prying into anyone else's love life.'

'Such as?'

His cousin whirled round to leave them.

'Such as burning the toast!' she answered lightly.

'Strange girl!' Angelo mused. 'We used to get on so well together, too.'

'Perhaps if you were to try harder you'd have more success,' Harriet advised. 'And now I really must go or I shall be late opening the shop.'

'Let me take you,' he offered, his mouth full of toast. 'It's practically on my way and you have all these parcels to carry.'

'Two,' Harriet corrected. 'Why not take Graziana as far as the college?'

'She has the Bugatti! Besides, I have a mind to see the shop in case I decide to work there.'

Surprised, she turned in the doorway to look at him.

'But we have no real need for another pair of hands,' she objected.

'Part-time, I meant. I could then get on with my photography when I felt like it. Rome is full of opportunities in that direction.'

'And full of photographers! You'd have far more scope on your grandmother's estate,' she advised.

He shrugged.

'It isn't really Grandmother's any more,' he said casually. 'Tarquin has practically taken over, don't you think?'

'I don't know. He hasn't exactly confided in me, but I do know that he needs help—the kind of help you could so easily give him,' Harriet declared.

'You make a staunch advocate on his behalf!'

'I appreciate how things are!'

'Then let me transport you and your precious parcels to the shop. It will do no harm.'

'Well, if you can change in five minutes.' She glanced at his ridiculous night attire. 'You certainly can't drive around Rome like that!'

Graziana watched them go, standing at the window in her dressing-gown, a deep frown marring her brow.

Harriet sat down in the car with the little bronze statuette on her knee, hugging the god of love between her hands.

'What have you got there that's so precious?' Angelo wanted to know as he turned the car into the Via Sistina, missing a passing bus by a hairsbreadth.

'Something Tarquin wants to sell.'

They were held up in the inevitable traffic jam around the Piazza di Spagna and he turned to look at her.

'Valuable?' he asked.

'I don't think I could have parted with it,' she said without answering the direct question.

'Is it family?'

She shook her head.

'It's—something Emmy Luciano wishes to sell. Apparently Tarquin gave it to her some time ago, so I should imagine it's quite valuable.'

'It wouldn't be the bronze Cupid, by any chance?' Angelo asked. 'Tarquin gave it to them as a wedding present—Emmy and Carlo!' His voice was suddenly harsh. 'She led him a pretty dance, you know.'

'I think she's changed a great deal in the past year,' Harriet managed to say as they crawled forward through the chaos of converging traffic into the *piazza* where the magnificent Santa Trinità dei Monti soared above them at the top of the Spanish Steps. 'She doesn't seem to want to come to Rome now unless it's absolutely necessary.'

'It's way out of character as far as Emmy is concerned.' Angelo paused to hurl a rude word at the driver of a motor-scooter who had cut across his path. 'But perhaps she likes being on the estate beside Tarquin all the time. I wonder if my grandmother knows.'

'Tarquin would tell her if he thought it necessary.'

'You have absolute faith in his integrity!'

'I think he wouldn't hesitate to tell the truth.'

'With the lack of reliable information rumours invariably multiply,' Angelo mused, obviously thinking of something else, 'but I don't think Tarquin would care what people said so long as he believed he was doing the right thing. He never did bother about public opinion.'

They edged their way slowly through the traffic, avoiding other drivers almost miraculously in the chaos that was early-morning Rome.

'If I'd walked from the Steps I could have been there by now,' Harriet pointed out.

'Such gratitude!' He turned the car into a side street where fruit vendors were unloading their wares at the back entrances of little secluded restaurants. 'Will you let me take you to lunch at one o'clock?'

'Please, Angelo,' she said, 'go back to Cerano. There's far more for you to do on the estate than here in Rome.'

'You give me no encouragement,' he declared, pulling up at a space beside the kerb. 'Don't forget the Cupid. I'd hate to think you didn't care about him!'

'*Will* you go back to the estate?' she asked, taking the parcels from him as she stood on the pavement. 'I think Tarquin needs you.'

He heaved an exaggerated sigh.

'You make it impossible for me to refuse,' he said. 'Thank goodness the Villa Ilena isn't too far away!'

Of course, he would come to Rome whenever the spirit moved him, Harriet thought as she turned away, but at least he would be on the estate some of the time, helping Tarquin at a busy time of the year.

She reached the shop to find Dino already there.

'I do not trust to buses or cars,' he declared. 'I walk. It is the only way in Rome.'

He must have come a very long way on foot because he lived on the far side of the Tiber somewhere off the Viale Giuseppe Mazzini in part of a house which he said had belonged to his grandfather. Already he had removed the dust-sheets from the counter showcases and was flicking a feather duster over their larger wares.

'I've something here I would like you to value,' Harriet told him, laying her precious burdens on the nearest glass-topped case.

Dino unwrapped both parcels while she took off her coat.

'This is exquisite!' he exclaimed, holding the Cupid up to the light. 'A connoisseur's piece.'

A lump had come into Harriet's throat.

'It has to be sold,' she said. 'It's something quite personal, but—but the owner needs the money.'

'A pity,' remarked Dino, caressing the little statue's wings. 'I would give a great deal to possess it, but it is far beyond my means.'

'How much do you think?' Harriet asked unhappily, because the little Cupid would have remained her most cherished possession if Tarquin had given it to her.

The price Dino mentioned was far beyond her slender means even if she had given way to the mad impulse to buy it.

'We'll put it in the window,' she said.

'It will go very soon,' Dino predicted. 'It's the sort of thing people buy.'

Strangers! People who really didn't care where the little Cupid had come from or what he had stood for long ago!

The bronze statuette remained in the window for over a week, however, without a purchaser. People came in to look at it more closely, but shook their heads and went out again, empty-handed.

'Perhaps we've priced it too high,' Harriet suggested.

'No price can be too high for love!' Dino smiled. 'You will see. Someone will buy it, sooner or later.'

At the beginning of the following week, when they were not quite as busy as they had been, a tall man made his appearance in the shop doorway.

'You seem to have very few customers this morning,' Tarquin said, closing the door behind him. 'I was in Rome, so I thought I would pay you a visit.'

Taken completely by surprise, Harriet could only look at him in silence.

'You look as if you've seen a ghost,' he said, smiling into her startled eyes. 'Did your customer return for the vases?'

'He was more than pleased with them.' She steadied her voice with an effort. 'I'm glad you've come, Tarquin. I wanted to ask you about the bronze statuette.'

'The Cupid?' His expression sharpened. 'I see he is still in the window.'

'Yes.' She avoided his gaze. 'I—wondered if I'd put too high a price on him.'

He prowled to the far side of the shop, seeming to give the matter some thought.

'I have half a mind to buy him myself,' he said, at last.

'Oh—would you?' Her eyes lit up. 'It would be nice to think of him at the Villa Ilena rather than in some museum or even in a private collection where he was just another *objet d'art*.'

'Why have you become so attached to him?' he asked in the most casual way.

'I don't know.' She was suddenly confused. 'I have really no right to interfere—to advise you one way or another.'

'No,' he said, and then quite suddenly: 'Emmy needs the money, but she wouldn't take it directly from me. That was why I asked you to arrange the sale for her.' He stood looking down at the array of silver in the showcase. 'Harriet,' he said, 'I owe you an apology.'

She looked at him questioningly.

'When you first returned to Rome,' he explained, 'I still believed that Angelo had gone with you when you left for England in such a hurry a year ago. I know now that you went alone.'

'I'm glad,' she said, drawing a deep breath of relief. 'I'd like the Contessa to know, too.'

'I've a feeling she already does.' He stood looking at her for a moment longer. 'The fact that my brother has returned means a great deal to her, although she doesn't think he will stay at the Villa Ilena for very long.'

'What do you think?' she asked, overwhelmingly glad that one misunderstanding, at least, had been swept away by Angelo's return. 'He's still keen on photography.'

'He could do that in his spare time.' He dismissed his brother's talent with a brief wave of his hand. 'The estate is for real, you know. It could be a solid investment as far as Angelo is concerned. I would take over the actual growing of the vines and the administration while he dealt with the overseas trade. De Filippo could remain a respected name in the wine trade even if it was run solely by the brothers Greymont!'

'You must speak to him,' she advised.

'I have already done so, but I gathered that I must wait for my answer.' His expression hardened. 'It's time he settled down, but perhaps I should agree to a spell in Rome for him so that he can finally make up his mind, one way or another.'

'What would he do?' Harriet asked, completely unprepared for his answer.

'He wants to come here, to work in the shop.'

'But he knows nothing about it!' she protested, vaguely disturbed by the suggestion.

'He could learn, and I can carry on quite well alone for at least a year.'

'Is that an irrevocable decision?' she asked quietly, wondering what she was going to do with Angelo in the offing all day long. 'Is it something you've thought about?'

'Very thoroughly. I know he's not going to settle on the estate right away when there are so many distractions in Rome, but it's entirely up to you. If you feel disinclined to cope with so much responsibility I shall understand.'

She hesitated, not wanting Angelo but wanting to help where she could.

'What does the Contessa say?' she asked.

'My grandmother will be pleased if she thinks he will stay in Italy,' he said. 'You will have to train him, of course, you and Dino between you, until she returns.'

'Tarquin, are you trying to say that she may not return?' she asked anxiously.

'We must think of that also,' he said. 'She is a very old lady, though an amazingly determined one.'

It all seemed to be falling into place as far as Harriet was concerned. There were two family businesses to consider, and if Angelo would not embrace the wine trade in the end at least he would have the alternative of the shop in one of Rome's most fashionable thoroughfares to fall back upon. The Contessa—or Tarquin—was feathering Angelo's nest for him and she could not blame them.

'I hope she will come back,' she said lamely, 'and meanwhile I'll help Angelo all I can.'

Tarquin stood with his back to her for a moment, as if he would add something more to what he had just said, and then he slid back the partition between the shop and the window and took out the little Cupid.

'I'll let you have a cheque,' he said, his mouth suddenly grim, 'and then you can parcel this up for me and keep it in the safe till I need it.'

The little statuette stood on the display case between them, wings outspread, bow in hand, an arrow already in place, but suddenly it seemed as if the arrow would never speed on its way. It was frozen there in shining bronze, never to leave the bow. Harriet put it hastily behind her.

'I'll attend to it later,' she promised, watching as Tarquin made out the necessary cheque. 'Will you return to Cerano right away?'

'Immediately,' he said. 'I have a buyer coming to look at some wine tomorrow.'

What had she hoped for? His company for only a day? What a fool she was, hoping and hoping like this! Tarquin was lost to her for ever and she must steel herself to accept the fact. Yet, only a moment ago, when he had made his straightforward apology, there had been something warm between them, a suggestion of understanding which could have swept away the past.

When she told Graziana the news about Angelo that

evening she was greatly surprised by the younger girl's reaction.

'I don't think it's at all a good idea to have Angelo in the shop,' she said bluntly. 'He'll only cause havoc and then we'll all be involved. Why doesn't Tarquin keep him at the villa and make him grow grapes?'

'I don't think anyone could force Angelo to do something against his will,' Harriet decided. 'He's too like the Contessa for that.'

'She'll be furious,' Graziana declared. 'She *wants* him at Cerano.'

'She wants him in Italy—anywhere,' said Harriet. 'She wants him to strike roots, Graz, and who can blame her? She's a very proud old lady who loves her country.'

'Like I love America,' said Graziana unexpectedly. 'I guess I ought to go back there.'

'What about your studies?'

Graziana thought for a moment,

'Maybe it would be a waste if I suddenly threw them up,' she agreed, 'but some day I'll go.' She prowled restlessly about the room. 'Some day I'll be forced to go back into the heart of my own family and be an all-American girl again. Can you imagine me settling down in Iowa after all this?'

'No, I can't,' Harriet answered truthfully, 'but you're only half-way to your diploma and I would leave it at that. You came here because you wanted to paint and now you've got what you want. It ought to be enough.'

'Why is it never enough?' Graziana said absently. 'We want the whole world to hold in our hands and love into the bargain.'

CHAPTER FIVE

It was another week before Angelo put in an appearance and then he came to the shop in the middle of the afternoon, asking where he could begin. A steady flow of customers had been in and out all morning, leaving Harriet slightly distraught, and the very last person she wanted to see was her new pupil.

'I'll find you something to do,' she promised, rearranging some of the items in the window which had been disturbed by the rush of customers. 'Perhaps you could stick on a few price-tags for me to begin with.'

'That will be hectic,' Angelo said dryly, picking up a tiny silver shoe which had been fashioned into a pin-cushion. 'Can't you just imagine the grand lady who first owned this exquisite piece of nonsense sticking pins in it all day just for the hell of it! Or this,' he added, selecting an elaborate ring with a hinged top. 'I bet the Borgias kept their deadly poison in it—a spot here and a discreet tap there and they wouldn't have an enemy in sight!'

'You have far too fertile an imagination,' Harriet said as the door opened to admit her first customer of the afternoon. 'You can work in the back shop,' she added firmly. 'Dino will show you the price lists.'

Angelo grinned at her.

'I think this is going to be fun,' he said.

Surprisingly, he worked with a will for the next few days. He had found suitable lodgings near the flat and parked his car next to Graziana's, so that they saw him most evenings, although sometimes he excused himself, saying that he had a photographic session at a friend's studio and would be late coming back. They heard him then, revving his engine under their window in an attempt to squeeze in at the curb, and Graziana would pull up the sash in a temper and tell him not to waken the whole neighbourhood at two o'clock in the morning. On these occasions they were wholly Italian, shouting reckless threats to each other until Angelo bowed off with a grin.

Their days were very full, and Harriet put the little Cupid safely away in the silver vault under the shop, trying to forget about him—and Tarquin.

It was not at all easy, but it was also surprising how quickly the days passed. On her first really free afternoon Harriet had all Rome to herself. Angelo had gone to Pisa to act as stand-in for a photographer friend who had suddenly obtained a more lucrative commission elsewhere and Graziana was sketching in the Casina Borghese, so she was free to please herself till the sun went down.

It was a great delight to her to wander around the ancient city among the ruins of a lost empire, wondering about the men and women who had once made it their home, and almost inevitably she found herself climbing the Palatine hill where she could look down on the Roman Forum and the ruined palace of the Flavians. The Temple of Venus and the mighty ruined circle of the Colosseum rose towering in the background with the roar of the traffic around it like the roar of the crowds who had watched the spectacles from its tiered terraces long ago. Here was the Rome of so many loves and hates, of desires and power and treachery, and above it all the ilex trees still rose in remote splendour, pointing dark fingers to the sky.

She sat on a ruined wall, the stone warm to her touch in the bright spring sunshine as it all seemed to come alive, and then, moving just beneath her, she became aware of a couple approaching beneath the trees. At first she failed to recognise them, and then she knew that it was Tarquin and Emmy Luciano walking arm-in-arm in earnest conversation. It was as if they were alone in the whole wide world, with nobody there to see. Emmy wore a pink dress with a silk scarf on her head, and she carried a little bouquet of flowers. Flowers that Tarquin could have bought for her earlier in the day!

Harriet struggled to her feet, drawing back to stand in the shadow of the broken wall. She wanted to run, to hide herself from the lovers' view, because who could pretend now that Tarquin and Emmy were not deeply in love?

The pink dress, the kerchief over Emmy's bright head and the bunch of flowers! Did they mean something else? Did they mean that Emmy and Tarquin had just become man and wife?

Sick in her heart, she clung to the ancient wall until they had passed, and then she ran into the nearby gardens to sit among the broken pillars of a lost empire, facing her own disillusionment. It could only mean one thing: some of the rumours which had swept Rome were undoubtedly true.

She found herself wandering the streets of the busy capital, pausing at last in the Piazza di Spagna and quite unable to remember how she had got there. The sun was shining, people were smiling and greeting one another, but she was desperately alone. She began to mount the famous Steps to the Santa Trinità dei Monti, pausing half way to look back down on the busy square. At the foot of the Steps the flower vendors had piled their scented wares—carnations, roses, lilies and violets, each a splash of brilliant colour against the pale stone of the gently-sloping stairway to the church, and she wondered if it had been here that Tarquin had bought Emmy the bouquet she had carried all the way to the Palatine hill.

As usual, the Steps were thronged with itinerant artists working in watercolour or charcoal and she stopped to watch as a portrait or a local scene took shape beneath their gifted hands. One in particular held her attention. He had sketched a girl with a dog, and it was so lifelike that she could hardly turn away. The artist himself was a hirsute young man, heavily bearded, with long hair reaching to his shoulders, but something about his eyes held her captive. They were sombre eyes, deeply set in his thin, bearded face and mirroring all the anguish she felt in her own deeply-wounded heart. Dark tragedy had stalked the mind behind them, leaving its traces in their shadow-haunted depths, and the mouth she could just see was thin and bitter. Unlike the other artists, he did not ask if he could draw her portrait. He sat there with the picture of the girl on his easel, gazing into space.

'It's beautiful,' Harriet remarked, looking down at the portrait.

He nodded.

'She will come for it this afternoon.'

He spoke quietly, turning away, and she saw how thread-bare his coat was. It had been a good coat, well-cut and from an excellent tailor, but no doubt he had inherited it from some generous benefactor, because it was too big for him. It hung on his thin shoulders like a cloak, making him look oddly distinguished in spite of his dishevelled state.

'You have a wonderful talent,' she remarked. 'I'm sure your sitter will be pleased with what you've done. The dog is so lifelike. How long does it take to finish such a portrait?'

The penetrating dark eyes searched hers for a moment as if the man would read her innermost thoughts.

'The dog was my greatest problem,' he said. 'It is difficult to make an animal sit still for any length of time.'

'I suppose it had to be absolutely accurate,' Harriet suggested. 'She looks as if she loves that dog.'

'I could not tell you so,' he answered, 'because I do not know. She sat for me for only one hour.' He drew a fresh canvas from a pile under his stool. 'If you will remain absolutely still I will sketch you as you are now.'

Harriet was ready to refuse when she suddenly remembered the look she had first seen in his eyes, the tortured, haunted look of a man very near to despair. Perhaps he needed the money more desperately than she imagined. She would pay for the sketch, of course, whatever he asked.

He worked very fast and when he had finished one sketch he laid it aside and started on another.

'Now you are more relaxed,' he said.

Harriet sat there, completely oblivious of the small

crowd which had gathered to watch while he finished the second drawing.

'They're—very good,' she had to admit. 'You—see me as I am.'

He turned away with a faint smile.

'That is a nice compliment,' he said.

'How much do I owe you?'

He waved her offer of payment aside.

'Please,' she insisted. 'You know I couldn't take your drawings for nothing, and I really do want them.'

He shrugged his meagre shoulders.

'Six thousand lire,' he told her indifferently.

'It isn't nearly enough,' she protested. 'They're quite professional.'

'It is all I ask,' he said, searching for a suitable piece of paper in which to wrap her purchase. 'Today I have been fortunate.'

'Are you here most days?' Harriet asked.

He shook his head, bending to his task.

'Not very often,' he said. 'I go from place to place, city to city. Tomorrow I may be in Perugia or even in Florence.'

She handed him the money he had asked for, sorely tempted to increase it but feeling that he would not accept charity. She might pay for his talent but nothing more, which meant that he was a proud man in spite of his shabby exterior.

'I think you ought to paint in oils or watercolour,' she told him.

'I do that also, on a commission, but mostly in Florence.' He was standing with his back to her, waiting for her to go. '*Arrivederci, signorina!* I hope you will be well pleased with your portrait.'

He had made a tremendous impression on her, Harriet realised as she walked away clutching the badly-wrapped sketches, but perhaps it was only because she had paused on the way up to the church of Santa Trinità dei Monti with her own world collapsing around her to look into his sorrow-haunted eyes and realise that she was not alone.

The man was a clever artist, but there were dozens of them in Rome hoping for a livelihood, she was forced to admit, yet the quality she had recognised in his drawings was rare.

She carried them back to the shop, propping them up on her desk while she made her usual round of the premises before she lowered the steel shutters on the windows for the night. It was her turn to lock up, but she seemed to be drawn back irresistibly to her own portraits. The unknown artist had put so much into the eyes, making them a disturbing mirror of her innermost feelings so that she saw pain there and protest which she would never have admitted even to herself.

The impulse to destroy them was strong in her for a moment. They were far too revealing to let anyone see. She picked them up, holding them away from her as she noticed the artist's scrawled signature in the left-hand corner for the first time. Sudden curiosity prompted her to look more closely, realising that it was not a signature, after all, so she would never really know his name. What she made out was three entwined initials linked together by the brief flourish of a charcoal pencil and almost undecipherable. C.R.S. or C.R.L., she decided, thinking that she would never know, one way or another. He had said that he wasn't a regular on the Steps, that he worked mostly in Florence, on commission, and that was the last she would hear about him.

Laying the drawings face down on the desk, she closed the shop door behind her, walking by the Via Babuino back to the crowded Piazza where the flower-sellers were packing up for the day and the tourists who had lingered over their English teas were filing out of Babington's to drift aimlessly in the general direction of their hotels.

Subconsciously she glanced up at the Steps, but her artist was nowhere to be seen. Perhaps she should have taken the sketches back to the flat to show them to Graziana, who was herself an artist, but something had prompted her to leave them hidden away in the shop instead.

She would have forgotten them altogether in the pressure of the next few days if Angelo hadn't discovered them while he was searching for a fresh supply of price-tags.

'What have we here?' he demanded. 'You've been having your portrait done!'

'Nothing quite so romantic,' Harriet assured him, half-angry because he had discovered her secret. 'They're just two random sketches I had done on the Steps the other day.'

'I like them,' he said, holding them up to the light. 'Some of these fellows are really talented. The trouble is there are so many of them around, all hoping to be recognised one day. But this fellow is really good.' He held the drawings from him for a better effect. 'The second one, I think,' he decided. 'The other one is too melancholy. It happens all the time with portraits, of course. It takes a genius to paint a smiling face.'

'Like the Mona Lisa's,' Harriet suggested.

'The Gioconda smile was the mirror of an unfathomable mind,' Angelo recalled. 'I'm not saying that your artist is in the da Vinci class, but he is good. Did you ask his name?'

'No.' She took the sketches from him, not quite sure why she was so reluctant to discuss them in depth. 'He scrawled his initials, but that was all.'

'Apparently he hasn't got much conceit of himself,' Angelo said. 'Which is unusual. I thought you might like to give me one.'

'Why should I? Having them done was only—an impulse on my part.'

He came across from the desk to stand beside her.

'Why don't I take you out for lunch?' he suggested.

'Because I never eat a heavy meal in the middle of the day and because we are really far too busy to go out together.'

'Dino could mind the shop.'

'I dare say, but if we have more than one customer at a time he gets flustered.'

'You're looking for an excuse!' he accused.

'I don't need to look for one. You know how busy we are.'

'I suppose it's all grist to the mill!' He sighed. 'Will you have dinner with me, then, after you have raked in all the profit you can for Tarquin?'

'Graziana and I are going to a concert,' she excused herself.

'Oh, come on!' He put his arm about her waist. 'Concerts can wait, or you can go tomorrow.'

'Graz has booked our seats. I can't let her down.'

'Do you always keep promises?' he demanded.

'I do my best, and this time I mean to. Angelo, we have a lot of work to get through,' she pointed out.

She freed herself from his encircling arm and he laughed.

'What makes you so prickly?' he demanded. 'You never used to be. Who else is going to the concert, since you won't break your promise?'

'As far as I know, we are going alone.'

'It's unbelievable!' His dark eyes flashed. 'Two of the prettiest *signorinas* in Rome going out without an escort!'

'Get on with your work!' She pushed the bundle of price tickets towards him. 'We've got masses of these if you happen to run out.'

Feigning hurt, he retired to the inner room where he worked diligently enough till lunch time.

'I'm not going to renew my offer,' he said. 'I'm going to lunch alone. I don't take kindly to being snubbed.'

'You don't like being refused is what you really mean,' Harriet laughed. 'Oh, Angelo, be fair! I'd come if it wasn't for the fact that Dino can't be left to do everything. You know that.'

'I don't. You sounded very much as if you didn't want to come,' he sulked. 'Are you waiting for someone else?'

'A customer or two!'

'Is that all?'

'Absolutely. Why should I lie to you?'

'No reason I can think of at the moment.' He gave her a

final, searching look. 'See you!' he said with mock indifference as he walked away.

Harriet watched him with a little smile touching her lips.
Tarquin would never make anything of Angelo unless he
took a firmer hand with him, she thought.

The shop was empty and she went through to the inner
room where Dino was polishing silver. It was his day for
changing the window display and he had already made a
comprehensive selection from the basement vault.

'I see you have sold the Cupid,' he said.

'Yes.' She hesitated, not quite sure whether she should
tell Dino that Tarquin had bought it in the end. 'It's at the
back of the safe. I—we've been asked to keep it there till it's
wanted.'

'I can't understand anyone wanting to part with it,' Dino
said. 'It is an excellent piece—so *delicato*. Many people
have stood to admire it while it was in the window. I hope
it has been bought by someone who will appreciate it.'

'I think it has,' said Harriet, deciding that it was perhaps
best to tell Dino the truth, after all. 'It hasn't gone out of the
family. Tarquin bought it when he was here last week, but I
don't think he wants to take it back to the villa just yet.'

Dino nodded, not trying to hide his satisfaction.

'I am glad,' he said. 'We sold it to him in the first place.'
He considered her information further. 'Perhaps he wishes
it as a present again,' he suggested.

'I don't know, Dino. He seemed to buy it on an impulse,'
Harriet said, remembering how forlorn the little Cupid had
looked as he had stood all alone in the window. 'I could, of
course, be mistaken.'

The bell which announced a customer took her hurriedly
into the shop.

'I'll cope, Dino,' she said. 'Finish your lunch.'

The girl who stood waiting at the counter was no stranger
to her.

'Emmy!' she exclaimed. 'I had no idea you were coming.'

'I was in Rome, so I decided to look in.' Emmy Luciano
smoothed the fair hair back from her forehead with a nerv-

ous hand. 'I hope you don't mind,' she added.

'Of course not.' Harriet tried to adjust her thoughts to the present instead of remembering that Emmy had on the same pink dress that she had worn that day on the Palatine hill. 'Can I get you something—a coffee or some wine?'

'I wondered if we could go out.' Even if she had wanted to Emmy could not hide the tenseness in her voice. 'I'm alone, you see, till Tarquin picks me up at five o'clock.'

It seemed that she could not bear to be alone, in Rome, at least.

'Could we talk here?' Harriet suggested. 'One or other of us has lunch in the shop at midday once the tourist season starts, and Angelo has just gone out.'

'I met him on the Corso,' Emmy smiled. 'He was buying flowers. Angelo does not change, does he? I think he must have a new *innamorata* because he looked very morose. Perhaps she had been unkind to him and he was trying to say it with flowers!'

'He'll get over his disappointment soon enough,' Harriet predicted. 'Angelo is the eternal lover, never daunted and never really in despair.'

'You know him well, I can see.' Emmy offered her a tentative smile. 'Harriet, I would wish us to be friends,' she said. 'Tarquin thinks that I am too much alone, shut up in the Villa Coralo most of the time. Could it be so, do you think?'

The anxious blue eyes searched hers and Harriet swallowed hard. Emmy—and Tarquin—were asking almost too much of her.

'When you're in Rome,' she managed to say, 'I'll be pleased to help you if I can.'

Emmy put both hands on the centre showcase.

'I also came to thank you for selling the Cupid for me,' she said. 'I didn't expect it to bring so much.'

Harriet stiffened.

'It was quite valuable,' she pointed out. 'A really exquisite piece.'

'I know.' Emmy looked distressed. 'It was difficult for

me to part with it. You see, Tarquin gave it to us as a wedding present and—it must have seemed so ungrateful of me to part with it, but I felt that I had burdened him with my financial troubles long enough.'

'I'm sure he understands.' Harriet busied herself with the few articles which Dino had already removed from the window. 'If you really would like to stay I'll make some coffee.'

'Let me help you,' Emmy offered, peeling off her gloves. 'I have all the time in the world.'

Dino took over in the shop as another customer came in and Emmy followed Harriet through the velvet curtains to the inner room.

'I suppose I should find something to do,' she said, looking round at the general disarray in which they worked behind the scenes, 'but I'm not exactly trained for a career. I was hopelessly spoiled by a doting father, Harriet, who had the temerity to die when I needed him most. That's why I depend so much on Tarquin,' she added thoughtfully. 'He's about the only other person I can trust.'

Skilfully she seemed to be avoiding any mention of her husband.

'What would you like to do?' Harriet asked as she made the coffee. 'In a city like Rome there must be some job you could tackle.'

Emmy stood still in the middle of the room.

'You were there that day,' she said emotionally, her thoughts far removed from their present environment. 'The day of the accident. How can I ever forget it, ever live it down? I was so crazy, so thoughtless, concentrating on nothing but my own amusement, but I loved Carlo. I always loved him, although I was foolish and wild, and now it can never be the same. We never get a second chance, do we? There's always some price to be paid. I would pay it gladly,' she rushed on, 'if I could turn back the clock, but that is impossible to do, is it not? Time never goes backwards: it goes marching on relentlessly, leaving us behind.'

'Sometimes we are given a second chance,' Harriet said

slowly. 'Being sorry afterwards isn't much good, but we can try to make amends.'

'I was so wayward, so *capricciosa*!' Emmy seemed determined not to spare herself. 'I ruined Carlo. He never had a lot of money and I spent as recklessly as I had always done. Then my father married for a second time and I had not his benefaction to draw on. He had a new wife to please and when he died he left most of his money to her. She was young, you see, and he had to take care of her, but I had very little to pay off my debts. Not as much as I expected.' She stared gloomily at the bright array of silver Dino had marshalled on the table. 'I took so much for granted,' she admitted. 'I thought nothing could ever change.'

'Don't distress yourself so much,' Harriet heard herself saying. 'Sometimes we have to put the past firmly behind us to—to cope with the future.'

'I am not like that,' Emmy confessed. 'I still long for what I cannot have. Oh!' she cried, 'I am such a misfortunate I deserve to die!'

Like most Romans she was an amalgam of gaiety and sophistication, kindness, exuberance and charm, and very Latin in all she said and did. Harriet did not believe for one moment that she wished to die, but she was suddenly conscious of a deeper side to Emmy, one she liked almost in spite of herself. There were traces of sadness in her make-up and a good deal of Italian fatalism as well as the proverbial detachment from the facts of everyday life, and she found them curiously endearing.

'Why don't you speak to Tarquin about finding a job?' she suggested. 'I'm sure he would help.'

Emmy shook her head.

'I can't burden him with my affairs all the time,' she objected. 'He thinks it best that I should remain at Cerano and I cannot tell him that I feel stifled there with nothing to do.'

It was obvious that she had been mistaken in her surmise that Tarquin and Emmy might already be man and wife, Harriet thought, but it did not mean that they would never marry. Emmy had been genuinely concerned about selling the little Cupid, which pointed to the fact that she cared what Tarquin might think and was reluctant to hurt him. If she had not actually forgotten Carlo that, too, was a point in her favour. 'I loved Carlo,' she had said. 'I always loved him.'

Surely Tarquin knew this and would respect her for it, and perhaps he was biding his time before he finally asked her to marry him.

'If you go to him and explain,' she said, 'I'm sure Tarquin will understand.'

'You do not know him,' said Emmy. 'He is very proud. He has offered me a home at the Villa Coralo because of his great friendship for Carlo and he would be angry if I flung it back in his face. He has also paid a good many of my debts and I cannot upset him by being ungrateful and offering to work. He did not wish me to part with the Cupid, but it was something I had to do.'

Harriet could not tell her that the little god of love was quite safe, hidden away in the silver vault beneath their feet. That must be Tarquin's secret, and no doubt he meant the statuette to remain there until he could give it back as a second wedding gift.

When they had finished their coffee and the spaghetti dish Dino prepared for them they waited for Angelo's return. He had never considered punctuality a matter of life and death, but four o'clock was striking before he put in a joyous appearance, bearing a rather dejected-looking bunch of flowers.

'For you, *signorina*!' he announced, planting an exuberant kiss on Harriet's cheek. 'All is now forgiven!'

'Where have you been?' Harriet demanded in exasperation. 'Do you realise what time it is?'

He glanced at his watch.

'It is almost ten minutes past four o'clock in the afternoon,' he declared, 'according to your crazy English time! In Rome it is sixteen hours and ten minutes, and I have been passing the time of day with a great friend on the Via

Veneto who will visit you as a customer before five o'clock!'

'Do I know him?' Harriet asked, realising how impossible it was to remonstrate with Angelo in his present mood.

'No, but you soon will. He is a most charming man, a true sophisticate, and he has a great deal of money. What is more important, he is a collector of rare books and was pleased to hear that we have re-opened my grandmother's shop.'

'When he arrives,' Harriet said dryly, 'I'll leave you to deal with him.'

Angelo looked round at Emmy, evidently not at all surprised to see her.

'You will notice how sadly I am rejected,' he sighed. 'Even my flowers are cast aside by this heartless English girl. I bring them as a token of love, but they are not accepted. What do you think I should do?'

'Put them in water,' Emmy advised wickedly. 'They will surely survive.'

'I do not think so. They hang their heads in utter dejection!'

'Give them to me,' said Harriet, 'and try to be sensible! You're only hoping to divert our attention from the fact that you're very late!'

'Life is a tragi-comedy,' Angelo declared. 'Why do we pretend that it is anything else? Harriet has broken my heart!'

'Angelo!' Harriet exclaimed. 'You're impossible! Get back to work. I've marked up some prices for you, so you ought to have plenty to do till your friend arrives. Be careful with the price-tags, won't you?'

'You think that I care nothing for this work,' he said more seriously as he turned towards the inner room, 'but I do. You help me and I am grateful. One day I will prove this to you.'

Harriet put the wilted flowers into a lustre jar, filling it to the brim as Emmy looked on. She had always loved flowers, hating to see them die for want of care, and she handled them with tenderness. When she had put them on a table by the window she looked up to see Emmy watching her with a puzzled expression in her blue eyes.

'You really are fond of Angelo,' she commented, 'and he was always a charmer. Tarquin is very pleased that he has returned home, and he would be happy to see him married and settled down.'

The statement seemed to match the look she had given them when Angelo had first proffered his faded flowers, making his outrageous statement about being rejected, and Harriet could not help wondering if she would retail the incident to Tarquin in due course.

'Do you think I might help?' Emmy asked when the first of the afternoon customers made their appearance. 'I could easily polish silver or even tie up the parcels when you have made a sale.'

Harriet hesitated.

'You wouldn't have to pay me,' Emmy rushed on. 'I could come whenever Tarquin was in Rome. It would be something to do and—a small return for everything he is doing for me.'

'Tarquin might not wish you to work in the shop,' Harriet objected.

'He wouldn't really mind. He wants me to feel—as free as possible,' Emmy told her.

'Well, you could help Angelo with the pricing.' Her acquiescence had been reluctant, Harriet realised. 'He's still rather slow.'

'Thank you, Harriet.' Emmy sounded almost too eager.

There were five customers in the shop when Tarquin finally made his appearance. Harriet saw him standing just inside the door, obviously looking for Emmy, and in case he would go away again she excused herself to the customer she was serving to cross to his side.

'Emmy's in the back room helping Angelo,' she explained. 'She asked to do something and I couldn't very well refuse.'

He frowned.

'Do you honestly need her assistance?' he asked.

'When we are busy an extra pair of hands is always acceptable,' she answered truthfully. 'Emmy didn't seem to think you would mind.'

'I have no right to "mind" what she does with her spare time,' he said, still frowning, 'and I suppose she has plenty of it. If it pleases her to work here and doesn't inconvenience you perhaps it might be a good idea if she were in Rome more often.' He hesitated, as if he were about to add something more specific, but he had to step aside as another customer opened the door. 'This must be your busiest time,' he said. 'I won't hold you up.'

The new customer was Angelo's friend from the Via Veneto.

'I'll call Angelo to attend to you,' Harriet said, following Tarquin into the back room.

'It's an absolutely splendid idea, don't you think?' Emmy was saying as she entered. 'It means that you won't have to feel so responsible for me all the time when we do come to Rome.'

Her voice was high-pitched and excited, the colour in her cheeks heightened as she waited for Tarquin's reply.

'I can't refuse you,' he said briefly as he laid a small package on the desk. 'These are the cameos we took to be cleaned,' he added as Harriet came forward. 'My grandmother priced them and sent them on to me. She feels that she can put them on the market now.'

Harriet's thoughts went rushing back to Sorrento and their wonderful drive through the Campania. It would never happen again because next time he would probably go with Emmy, driving on to Amalfi where their love affair had first started.

She gathered up the cameos, some of which were mounted in antique silver, others in gold.

'They should sell quite quickly,' she decided, fingering the necklace of tiny cameos which she wore round her own neck.

The necklace was like an amulet, she thought, although Tarquin had given it to her in gratitude and not from love.

He saw the almost protective little gesture and smiled, but did not comment.

'Perhaps you would like to come to the opera with us,' he suggested. 'I have a spare ticket which it would be a shame to waste.'

'Harriet has just turned me down,' Angelo looked up from his pricing to say. 'You will have to try again some other time, Tarquin.'

'It was Emmy's idea,' his brother said, gazing at the flowers Harriet had arranged in the lustre jar. 'Perhaps another time.'

If only Angelo had explained that she was going out with Graziana, Harriet thought, leaving them to go back to her customers, although what difference it would have made to Tarquin was hard to see.

At seven o'clock, when all Rome seemed to be drifting towards the Via Veneto, she prepared to close the shop. The last of her customers had departed and Emmy and Tarquin had gone off to the Trastevere to dine. Obviously they were staying in one or other of the hotels in the vicinity, since they were going to the opera. Angelo lingered in the shop doorway.

'I'll see you safely home,' he offered, 'though you don't deserve my continuing solicitude!'

'I must unpack the cameos Tarquin brought.' Suddenly Harriet wanted to be alone. 'I'll put the prices down on your list and you can mark them in the morning.'

'I'll wait,' he said doggedly.

Hastily she scribbled down the prices Tarquin had recommended, adding them to the list Angelo was working on. The silver-mounted ones were cheaper, the gold filigree more expensive. She handed over the keys as she went to get her coat.

'Are you forgetting my flowers?' Angelo demanded.

'Of course not!' She had completely forgotten them. 'They're quite revived now.'

As they locked up she became aware of a shadowy figure in the background and she glanced apprehensively at the barred windows, but the man moved quickly away, melting into the shadows of the side street as they followed him round the corner. The tall, bearded figure was disturbingly familiar, but perhaps she had been thinking too much about the artist who had sketched her portrait on the Spanish Steps.

'You'll have to change,' Graziana informed her when she finally reached the flat. 'It's quite a grand concert, so everyone will dress up. Was that Angelo who brought you back?' She glanced at the flowers.

'What shall I wear?' Harriet asked, evading the leading question. 'As if I didn't know!' she laughed. 'My grey chiffon—or else!'

'You have that pretty pink thing you haven't worn yet,' Graziana reminded her, gazing gloomily at the bouquet.

'Not pink,' Harriet decided hastily. 'I want to wear my cameos.' She was thinking about Emmy in the pink dress she had worn on the Palatine hill. 'They stand out so well against the grey chiffon.'

'Why do you encourage Angelo?' Graziana demanded, still gazing at the flowers. 'He bought them for you, I suppose.' She turned quickly, the cool American miss transformed into the passionate *signorina*. 'He is not for you!' she declared sullenly. 'What would you say if I told you that he was the one who was really responsible for the accident at Amalfi that day? He was having one of his usual mild affairs, with Emmy this time, and he was playing the fool in the speedboat. He could have saved Carlo when it overturned, but he chose to help Emmy who was not in any real danger because she was also a good swimmer. It was Tarquin who was blamed for Carlo's death and he didn't contradict the rumours. He covered up for Angelo because he knew how much it would distress my grandmother to know how foolish Angelo had been.'

'It can't make any difference now,' Harriet said unhappily. 'Emmy and Tarquin are in love with each other.'

It was a disappointing evening for them both. The Auditorium was full of the usual happy crowd, but Har-

riet's thoughts quickly strayed from the Via della Con-
ciliazione to the Via Viminale where Emmy would be sitting in her pink dress or in something equally pretty listening to the opera with Tarquin by her side.

Graziana, too, was in a restless mood.

'I didn't enjoy it one bit,' she declared as they came away
from the concert. 'They were all too tense—trying too
hard.' She walked so quickly that Harriet had difficulty in
keeping up with her. 'Are we being followed?' she asked.

Harriet glanced behind her.

'Not unless you count the rest of the audience!'

'I meant that man over there on the opposite pavement,'
her companion explained. 'He was standing at the door as
we came out. He looked as if he wanted to speak to you.'

'You have too vivid an imagination!' Harriet could just
make out a tall, bearded figure hurrying away. 'If he *had*
wanted to speak he would have come across, but——'

'Yes?'

'He's rather like my artist—the man who did my portrait
on the Steps the other day.'

'Perhaps he thinks he sold you the sketches too cheaply,'
Graziana suggested, hailing a taxi. 'We'd better give him
the slip.'

The bearded man had merged into the shadows, but
that second, disturbing glimpse of him in one day was
difficult to forget. Once he had been outside the shop, and
here he was again, near the concert hall almost as if he had
been waiting for them to come out.

Artists were so confusingly alike, of course, and it could
be no more than a coincidence, but if she had been able to
look into his eyes Harriet thought that she could have been
sure.

CHAPTER SIX

WHEN she reached the shop the following morning she took the sketches from the desk to look at them again. They were really amazingly good, she decided, but they were also disturbing because they revealed so much. The artist had caught more than just a likeness, giving her secret away for all who cared to see. Her eyes were the deep mirror of her love, the contours of her mouth the reflection of her pain.

On an impulse she was about to tear them up, but the sound of the shop door opening made her lay them aside. It was early for a first customer, but trade had been good all week and she hurried through the velvet curtains to confront Tarquin with an enquiring smile.

'Oh!' she exclaimed, looking beyond him for Emmy. 'I had no idea you would come back.'

'Did you enjoy your concert?' he asked, ignoring her surprise. 'The morning papers give it rave reviews.'

'I—it may have been a bit beyond my depth,' she confessed breathlessly. 'I thought it rather heavy. So did Graziana.'

'Graziana?' His eyebrows shot up. 'So that was who you were with?'

'Do you find it very strange?' she asked.

He laughed outright.

'Not at all. It was just the thought of Graziana finding time to go to the Auditorium which amused me.'

She waited, wondering why he had come.

'Harriet,' he asked, 'would you take Emmy under your wing for a week or two if I had to go abroad?'

'I've already done that,' she pointed out, allowing her indrawn breath to escape with a rush. 'You said you didn't mind her coming here to work, and I'm quite prepared to teach her all I can.'

'It would be better if she stayed in Rome while I was away,' he said. 'The Villa Coralo is completely isolated and she has no transport. Since—the accident she has been nervous about driving a car, and the Roman traffic is no great help.'

'Where would she stay?'

'Where she is now. At the Hotel Belvedere.'

She turned to the desk.

'Emmy must have plenty of friends in Rome,' she suggested.

'Indeed,' he agreed. 'But she is not quite ready to pick up the threads again. Not just yet. She is so easily reminded of the past.'

'I'll do what I can.' Harriet stared down at her own reflection in the charcoal sketches lying on the desk. 'I can't promise complete immunity, though. Emmy is bound to remember that I was also there, in the other boat.'

'Yes,' he said, coming up behind her. 'But she seems to think that you understand her better than most people, certainly better than the people she used to know.' He took up the nearest drawing, examining it closely. 'A good likeness,' he murmured. 'Where did you have it done?'

'In the Piazza di Spagna. One of the artists sitting on the Steps had been drawing a girl with a dog and I stopped to admire it. The sketch was very well done, and he went on to do these two of me.'

His eyes narrowed as he took up the second portrait, although this time he did not seem to be assessing the artist's work.

'Do you mind if I keep this?' he asked. 'It is an amazing likeness.'

What could she say? The words seemed to be dried up in her mouth, yet she knew that he could not want her portrait from any personal need. Why, then had he asked for it? Why, indeed!

Dino came in, fresh from his early morning walk, and Tarquin folded the sketch to put it in the pocket of his coat.

'I'll let you know about Emmy,' he said.

It was over a week before Harriet saw him again and during that time word came to say that the Contessa was about to return to the Villa Ilena. She had decided that she was well enough to come north for a while, although she would not be able to work in the shop. She would convalesce on the estate, visiting Rome occasionally now that the weather had improved.

Harriet received the news with a sense of shock. The Contessa was coming home, so what would Tarquin do about Emmy?

Thinking how involved she had already become, she waited for him to contact her, but the week passed without any message from him. Angelo had sold most of the cameos and Dino had been obliged to replenish their stock from the vault as their stock in the window display attracted buyer after buyer in the spring rush to the shops. She was modestly proud of her achievements, hoping that Tarquin would acknowledge how conscientiously she had worked in his absence.

When he came she was out. Dino had been told of a sale at a villa just outside the city and she had taken a taxi along the sunlit Appian Way to attend it in the hope of picking up a bargain or two, but prices were high and she had not been particularly successful. She returned to the shop feeling that her morning had been wasted to find Tarquin waiting for her. He looked tense and impatient as they confronted one another.

'I've been going through these,' he said, tossing a bunch of sales checks on to the counter in front of her. 'Do you realise that you have been selling the cameos at a giveaway price?'

Hot and tired, she glared back at him.

'It was the price you suggested,' she pointed out.

'For the silver-mounted ones,' he allowed. 'The gold

filigree is quite a different matter. Two of them have already gone.'

'That's impossible! I priced them myself.'

What she meant was that she had scribbled down a price for Angelo to copy in the morning and had thought no more about it.

'You're not giving me credit for a lot of intelligence,' she protested. 'I know the difference between gold filigree and silver.'

He regarded her coldly.

'It could have been a mistake,' he suggested.

'But you don't think so!' Her nerves were suddenly on edge. 'You would prefer to call it carelessness on my part.'

She could have told him that she hadn't sold the gold-mounted cameos, that she would have noticed the mistake immediately if she had, but the fact that he seemed to distrust her kept her silent.

'Harriet, I'm not accusing you,' he said tightly. 'I know how busy you have been and how easily these things can happen.'

'But you think I have been careless? That's what you are trying to say, isn't it?' Angry tears gathered in her eyes. 'In short, you think I've fallen down on the job, just as I did once before.'

'You're quite wrong.'

'Am I? You thought I had walked out on your grand-mother and everyone else when I went away a year ago, but I have told you why I went. The only thing I haven't told you is why I came back. I thought—I thought everything would be the same, that I'd be a respected member of this firm and trusted above everything else. Well, it doesn't seem to be like that at all.' She fumbled with the necklace she wore round her neck. 'I want you to have this,' she said. 'It might help to defray your loss over the cameos. I want it to go into stock.'

She laid the necklace he had given her on the display case between them, completely shaken by the thought that he had been so quick to distrust her. She knew that Angelo must have sold the cameos after copying down tne price of the silver ones, but she couldn't tell him so because it could so easily trigger off a confrontation between the brothers and Angelo was quite likely to throw up everything and go off again into the blue as he had done before, which would distress the Contessa and disillusion Tarquin even more. Why do I bother so much about this family? she wondered as she waited for Tarquin to speak.

'Don't be so foolish,' he said. 'Your necklace is three times as valuable as all the cameos put together.'

She had suspected as much and wondered why he had given it to her out of gratitude.

'That's beside the point,' she heard herself saying. 'I want to put it into stock. I have no real use for it.'

Her tone was clipped and decisive and he stood looking at her for a full minute before he gathered up the necklace and slipped it into his pocket.

'As you wish,' he agreed. 'I thought you wore it rather a lot.'

All the time, Harriet thought. Close over my heart, because you gave it to me one wonderful day as we drove through the Campania forgetting everything but each other.

Of course, it wasn't true. Even then he must have been thinking about Emmy and their future together, planning to make her his wife when all the gossip had cooled down.

'Angelo says the Contessa is coming home. It must mean that she feels a lot better,' she said formally as she pretended to busy herself with the morning mail.

'That's part of my reason for being here,' he said, making a quick circuit of the shop floor. 'I'm on my way to Capri to collect her. She has so many belongings that some of them will have to come by sea, but at least she can travel comfortably in the car.' He hesitated. 'We will have to arrange some sort of homecoming for her at the villa. I wondered if you could go there.'

The request took her completely by surprise.

'What about Emmy?' she challenged.

'Emmy is in Rome. I brought her this morning,' he explained. 'She feels that she would like to stay here for a while.'

'But surely she would be far better equipped to arrange your grandmother's homecoming than I would,' she protested. 'She knows the estate so well.'

He stopped his pacing at the far end of the showcase.

'I think you would do it better,' he said. 'Take Graziana with you, and perhaps even Angelo might spare a weekend to welcome her home.'

Harriet longed to return to the Villa Ilena, although it would probably tear her heart apart to ride through the estate again.

'What would you want us to do?' she asked, including Graziana for her own protection.

'Oh, the usual things,' he decided. 'The feminine touches, I suppose I mean. Flowers in all the rooms and so on. You know about that better than I do. The estate workers will want to do something on their own, of course. They are very fond of her, but you can safely leave these preparations to Enrico. His daughter is arranging for extra staff to be engaged, so you will have no more to do than supervise.'

She stood looking at him, not knowing what to say. He was asking her to perform a duty which was surely Emmy's, but he had not hesitated to do so.

'I'll speak to Graziana,' she offered, 'unless you have already done that?'

He shook his head.

'I thought I would leave it to you,' he said, 'but I don't think you will have much trouble with Graziana. She likes the life on the estate in spite of all she says about it, and she is very fond of Grandmother.'

'When will you come back?'

He considered the point.

'On Monday,' he said. 'It's a holiday, so you can wait at the villa till we arrive. If Angelo isn't there for any reason I'll drive you back to Rome.'

Graziana accepted the plan with her usual enthusiasm.

'We can go on Friday evening,' she suggested. 'Angelo and Dino can manage the shop between them on Saturday. It'll be a slack day when Monday is a holiday. Then Angelo can drive down on Saturday evening or even on Sunday. Did Tarquin say anything about Emmy?' she asked, frowning.

'She's in Rome.'

'Hidden away for the time being,' said Graziana uncharitably. 'Grandmother never approved of her, you know. She takes likes and dislikes to people, which she puts down to intuition, but I guess it's just because of Tarquin. She would *not* like to see him married to Emmy. Heigh-ho!' she sighed. 'What a family we are, to be sure! What do you plan to do at the villa?'

'I thought you might come up with a few suggestions,' Harriet said. 'You know the routine better than I do.' She was about to say that she had suggested Emmy in the same capacity, but thought better of it. 'Surely it has happened before.'

'I've never been in at the planning stage,' Graziana reflected, 'but we'll think of something. There'll have to be a dinner in the evening and some sort of reception committee from the estate workers to make a speech. She'll expect that. It's rather like a queen coming home after a long absence, isn't it? Everybody on parade, pulling their socks up, and all that! She'll expect reports and ask you all about the shop if Tarquin hasn't already told her all she wants to know.'

Wondering what sort of report Tarquin would make on her stewardship, Harriet prepared for the weekend in a mixed frame of mind.

'Don't tell me you're going to leave me in sole charge of the shop after the bloomer I made with the cameos,' Angelo remarked when she outlined their plans to him.

'Dino will be here,' she pointed out, 'and I've gone over most of the prices again. The mistake was as much mine as yours, Angelo. I wrote the prices down in too great a hurry. I should have been more specific about the gold mountings.'

'Not to worry!' he said cheerfully. 'It was no more than a fleabite!'

'Will you come to the villa to welcome the Contessa?' she asked eagerly, knowing how much it would mean to her employer.

'Since you ask me,' he said. 'It will be a change from Rome,' he added, pacing restlessly about the inner room. 'Do you honestly think I'm cut out for this kind of work?' he demanded.

'I think you should give it a longer trial, but if it doesn't work out you could always go back to the estate,' she suggested.

'Tramping grapes isn't much in my line, either.'

'They're not tramped nowadays,' she pointed out. 'They're pressed, which is much more hygienic.'

'But nothing so picturesque. Perhaps that's the trouble. Everything is mechanised now and there's no spontaneity. We don't sing at our work any more.'

'I've heard you singing in here!'

'Not for long. Dino can put a stop to it with a look!' Angelo declared. 'Besides, a shop isn't exactly the place to lift the roof off when you're bursting with joy and feel like singing.'

'Save it for the Villa Ilena,' said Harriet, overjoyed that he had agreed to return for the Contessa's homecoming.

Graziana picked up her brushes and easel early on the Friday afternoon, arriving at the shop shortly after four o'clock.

'I thought we might get away before the weekend rush,' she explained, 'but I suppose most of them will be on their way to the beaches in such glorious weather.' She looked half inclined to change her mind about going to Cerano. 'Maybe we could take our swim suits and bathe in the lake, though. It should be warm enough at this time of the year.'

The lake where Emmy had walked in the sun with her dog!

Harriet gave her last-minute instructions to Dino, warning Angelo to ask if he wasn't sure about prices.

'I'll do my best,' he promised, following them out to the taxi which was waiting to take them to the station because the Bugatti had succumbed to old age and refused to start. 'See you soon!'

The train was hot and stuffy, but the journey was soon over.

'We'll have to find another cab,' said Graziana. 'You wait here with the luggage and I'll see what I can do.'

Harriet drew in a deep breath of the keen mountain air. The hills were all about her, rolling majestically to the blue horizon, with little vineyards at their feet. Laurel, roses and bougainvillea climbed over garden walls and the powerful scents of spring filled the air with fragrance. Her heart rose on a wild surge of happiness, yet she was only going to prepare a welcome for her employer, something which Tarquin could have entrusted to the servants just as well.

Graziana returned with the hired car.

'He's a troubadour!' she announced, indicating the dark-eyed youth who jumped from behind the steering-wheel to help them with their luggage. 'This is going to be fun!'

The driver, whose name was Edoardo, had a light tenor voice and almost before he had re-started the engine they were engulfed in song. His repertoire was endless and very soon they were joining in the songs they already knew and learning others which he was happy to teach. He came from Napoli, he informed them, where to live was to sing!

The distance to the Villa Ilena seemed far too short. They reached the edge of the plantations, rolling up the long, straight drive to the tune of a rumbustious boat song, and when they reached the Villa the old stone walls seemed to waken from their sleep to listen to Edoardo's music with a startled air.

Even Enrico had heard their joyful approach, coming to the door in his long green baize apron with a yellow polishing-cloth in his hand and a warm welcome in his toothless smile.

'Enrico, here we are!' announced Graziana. 'I hope you were expecting us.'

He said that he had been expecting them all day, although it was obvious that he had been caught in the act of dusting off the last of the cobwebs.

Harriet paid off the taxi-driver.

'Probably we have the same rooms as before,' said Graziana, leading the way up the familiar staircase where the dust-cover had been removed from the magnificent carpet and the shrouds had been taken from the marble busts and urns which occupied the deep niches in the walls. The Villa Ilena had come alive, waiting for the return of its mistress.

Tarquin had set all the necessary wheels in motion before he left, and Enrico's attractive daughter came to ask if they had everything they needed, lingering expectantly in the doorway of Harriet's room to see the latest fashion from Rome. The estate workers were arranging a small carnival on Monday, she confided, to welcome back a loved employer, and already they were gathering flowers to make a traditional carpet on the terrace steps. Later, there would be fireworks under the stars.

'We'll miss the fireworks,' Graziana pointed out, 'if we go back to Rome.'

'You will be expected to stay,' Harriet suggested. 'You're family, and you have an extra day's holiday, anyway. Angelo can drive me back to Rome.'

'If he turns up,' Graziana reflected. 'I wish he wasn't so unpredictable. I know he loves being here and it's only staying power he lacks, but when is he going to realise that, can you tell me?'

They worked hard the following day, collecting flowers to arrange in the main *sala* and the ante-rooms until the lovely Renaissance villa came into its own again. Under a full moon, on the last night before Renata de Filippo came home, it gleamed like some fairytale palace among the tall ilex trees which surrounded it, quietly waiting for her return. Shadows as black as ink lay between the marble columns of the loggia, but the moonlight had turned the fountains to silver and nightingales sang their hearts out in the shelter of the orchard at the far side of the house.

Because Angelo failed to put in his expected appearance by nightfall, Graziana had become unnaturally quiet as they had ridden back among the vines from their afternoon exercise. They had gone as far as the lake where the Villa Coralo stood in sunny isolation among its sheltering orange trees, but she had not mentioned Emmy nor suggested that they might bathe, as she had done in Rome. Her impatience with her cousin mounted as the hours fled away, but she worked with a will and had even managed to produce a lovely watercolour of the Villa Ilena to present to her grand-mother when she arrived.

'She'll love it,' Harriet said. 'It's something very personal.'

They were seated in the loggia looking out over the moon-blanched garden when Angelo finally arrived, driving up to the terrace steps in a cloud of dust and petrol fumes.

'Welcome!' said Graziana stiffly. 'You're just in time.'

'Well, I made it,' he said, taking the marble steps two at a time. 'I never thought I would.'

'What happened?' Harriet asked.

'Everything! You're not going to believe this, but I broke down twice on the way.'

'You—or the car?' Graziana asked sarcastically.

'The car. It's really past its best.'

'What about yesterday?' his cousin demanded, in ruthless pursuit of the truth.

'I had something important to see to.' He avoided their concentrated gaze. 'I couldn't get away.'

'I suppose you are in dire need of something to eat,' Graziana suggested.

'I'm starving! Do you think Enrico would oblige?'

'At this late hour I'd rather you asked him than me!' Graziana rose to her feet. 'I'm off to bed. We have an early start in the morning.'

Harriet rang the pull-bell at the side of the *sala* mantel-piece.

'It really is too bad of you leaving it so late,' she scolded.

Angelo followed her into the room.

'I couldn't help it—honestly,' he apologised. 'I *did* break down and I *was* too busy on Saturday. I couldn't have got here before midnight.'

'It's almost midnight now.'

'I know, and I'll fast till morning, if you like,' he said in his most contrite voice. 'I really am sorry.'

Harriet accepted his apology, only too pleased that he had put in an appearance in time.

'I think we should go to the kitchens and see what we can forage for ourselves,' she suggested. 'Everyone seems to be in bed.'

The dark-eyed Maria appeared in the doorway, however, with a tray already in her hands.

'I heard you come,' she told Angelo with a happy smile, 'and I knew you would be hungry.' Maria, too, was glad that he had come home in time to welcome his grand-mother. 'You can sleep late tomorrow morning after your so long journey,' she promised.

There was no hope of Angelo or anyone else 'sleeping late' the following morning, however. Everyone seemed to be awake at cockcrow, putting the finishing touches to their efforts, and by midday a magnificent carpet of flowers adorned the terrace steps. The experts had been at work since first light, fashioning the intricate pattern with tiny flower-heads so that it would be complete in the minutest detail for the Contessa's arrival.

Harriet stopped to inspect it with a lump in her throat. It must be wonderful, she thought, to command so much respect and love.

By four o'clock most of the estate workers had gathered in the villa garden, forming two straggling lines on either side of the carriageway. They were all attired in their best clothes, the men with highly-polished boots and hats set straight on their heads, the women in wide, colourful skirts with white blouses under their embroidered bodices and flowers in their hair. All the children carried little posies to fling into the car when the Contessa appeared.

The whole scene was completely feudal in its simplicity, and under the blue sky it seemed just right. The backdrop of the ancient villa, the dark ilex like spears rising above the paler orchard trees, the gleaming columns festooned with honeysuckle and bougainvillea of every hue and the fountains whispering in the still air suggested a peace which might last for ever, and somehow Harriet knew that this was what Tarquin wanted to preserve.

The children were first to hear the approaching car, running to meet it as it came slowly along the drive. This was how Filippo brides must have come home over the years, Harriet thought, and this was how Tarquin would bring his wife to the Villa Ilena one day.

The Contessa sat in the open car as the children threw their flowers, and somehow she looked the happiest woman in the world. Her eyes were shining like a young girl's and her smile embraced everybody in sight. Treading carefully over the flower-carpet, she came up the terrace steps to where they were waiting.

'Angelo! Graziana!' she exclaimed, embracing her grandchildren. 'You give me great pleasure.'

'Nonna!' Graziana smiled, kissing her on the cheek.

The old lady turned to Harriet.

'Tarquin said you would be here.' Her smile was affectionate. 'You will stay, of course, until tomorrow to watch the fireworks display with us. Tarquin says it will be quite spectacular.'

'The shop——' Harriet began, but the Contessa waved her protest aside.

'Dino can attend to the shop for one day,' she decided. 'It's not often that I have my family here at one time.'

The estate foreman made a speech and they drank wine together while the children were shepherded off to the kitchens for cake and Coca-cola, which was something of a novelty to them. When they finally went away the Contessa sank back in her chair, laying her ebony stick aside as she took off her ceremonial hat.

'Here we are,' she said, 'back home!'

As soon as it was dark enough the fireworks display would begin, and then, when it was all over, they would dine together in the long room facing the terrace gardens. Harriet felt her excitement mounting as she laid her chiffon dress on her bed, wondering what to wear with it now that she no longer possessed the cameo necklace. The single string of pearls she owned was too pale, her gold chain not quite right. I'll go without, she thought, studying her reflection in the oval mirror which hung above her dressing-chest. Red hair is quite enough!

Slipping her feet into the grey satin pumps she had bought in Rome, she went slowly down the marble staircase as the telephone rang. Someone already in the study rose to answer it and she knew that it was Tarquin. There was a long silence after he gave his name.

Trying not to eavesdrop, she moved away, wondering if there was anything left undone. The central hallway was a bower of flowers, roses and lilies and carnations of every hue banked against shiny laurel and trailing honeysuckle, while pale gardenias stood in little tubs on the floor as they had come from the gardens. It was such a fitting setting for the gracious lady of the house, a true and lovely welcome home.

Suddenly there were tears in Harriet's eyes. Was Emmy going to spoil it all?

Tarquin came from the study, a look of frustration in his eyes as he walked across the decorated hall to where she was standing in the open doorway.

'It's lovely outside,' she said awkwardly. 'An ideal night for the display.'

He stood for a moment without answering.

'There's—nothing wrong?' she asked. 'No delay?'

'Nothing.' He was obviously considering something other than the fireworks. 'Harriet, I'd like to talk to you for a moment.'

He closed the heavy door behind them as they walked out into the starlit night.

'Yes?' she asked when they had reached the foot of the terrace steps.

'I want you to befriend Emmy,' he said in a tone so harsh that she hardly recognised it as his. 'She needs help.'

She turned to him, aghast that he should make such a demand on her.

'How can I?' she protested. 'How can I without feeling an utter hypocrite?'

Instantly his hand shot out, holding her arm in a vice-like grip.

'Perhaps it's time I told you the truth,' he said grimly. 'Carlo isn't dead. He has been seen in Rome.'

A surge of overwhelming relief was her first reaction, to be replaced immediately by the realisation of what his words could mean. She had already seen frustration in his eyes and there must be a gnawing despair in his heart as he contemplated his own future.

'That's where I go when I leave the estate,' he added. 'Not to any illicit rendezvous with my friend's wife.'

'I'm sorry,' she managed. 'If there's anything I can do to help, please tell me.'

'Emmy trusts you, which is more than she can say for her former women friends. They were a shallow lot and they dropped her like a hot potato when the scandal broke.' His contempt for Emmy's former acquaintances was complete. 'She had nobody to turn to.'

'Except you.'

'It was something I had to do,' he said. 'Then I realised how much Emmy had changed—wanted to change. The police enquiries were anything but a pleasant experience for her, especially when they came to the conclusion that Carlo hadn't drowned that night, after all. In spite of their intensive searching, no body was ever found, so Carlo's name was added to their list of missing persons and there the matter has rested until a week ago.'

'They've found him?'

He shook his head.

'Not yet.' His mouth firmed into a straight line. 'It's my intention to get there first. Whatever reason he had for—going off like that, I've got to bring him back. He was up to his eyes in debt, of course, and he had rowed with Emmy more than once about overspending, but that was no real reason for him to disappear. He should have considered the consequences for all of us. I know there's a time when things just blow up in your face, when there doesn't seem to be much point in going on, but it must have been pretty serious when Carlo opted out. I think he did it on the spur of the moment that night after the speedboat capsized. It was the ideal opportunity, and he took it. I think he swam to the shore and climbed the rocks and got away.'

Harriet shivered. Suddenly the night seemed very cold.

'Do you think you'll find him?' she asked.

'I think he has to come back if he is ever to live with himself again.'

In the pale starlight his mouth looked harder than ever. He hadn't said that he was not in love with Emmy and a whole mountain of complications seemed to rise ahead of him.

'What will you do?' she asked.

'Go on searching.' He hesitated, as if he had something in mind which concerned her. 'I think you may be able to help me.'

'Yes?' The word was no more than a whisper in the quiet night. 'I will if I possibly can.'

'Those sketches you had done on the Spanish Steps,' he reminded her. 'I took one of them because I thought I recognised the artist's signature. It was only initialled, but the letters tallied, although the writing was not the same. That could have been deliberate, of course, but, looked at another way, the letters could be C.S.R. and not C.S.L.' He led her further along the terrace as the moon appeared over the ridge of the hills. 'Can you describe him?' he asked urgently.

'He was tall and very thin, and he had a beard. His hair

was long, too, and unkempt. He wasn't at all like Carlo as I remember him,' Harriet decided, her pulses racing as she remembered her first encounter with the man on the Spanish Steps.

'A beard can change a man out of all recognition,' he said. 'What about his clothes?'

'They were very shabby, but I think they had once been quite expensive.'

'Did you notice a ring?'

She shook her head.

'It was his eyes I noticed most. I find it difficult to remember what Carlo looked like in any detail. It's just that——'

'Yes?' he demanded.

'There was a sort of suffering in his eyes. No, I don't think he was at all like Carlo,' she concluded.

'I've got to make sure,' he said. 'Carlo was a clever amateur painter and he could have taken to sketching in the Piazza when he had no other source of income to fall back on. He left all he had for Emmy.'

'He said that he often went to Florence, painting on commission,' Harriet remembered.

Tarquin's expression sharpened as the first of the fireworks shot into the air, burning in a yellow star-burst against the night sky to challenge the rising moon.

'I must go back there,' he said. 'Meanwhile, I will return your portrait and we will say nothing to Emmy. She has just phoned me after another disappointing day searching for clues. That is her real reason for being in Rome.'

Burst after burst of gleaming fire rose from the surrounding vineyards, dazzling the sky and bringing the others out to the terrace to watch. The swish of rocket after rocket filled the air with sound, to be followed by the bright cascades of light which shamed the moon. Harriet stood by Tarquin's side as a myriad artificial stars showered down upon them, only obliterated when they fell into the lake or died amid the garden trees. It was a wonderful homecoming for the Contessa, one that she hoped Tarquin would not spoil by discussing Emmy's future with his grandmother quite so soon.

It was late before they finished their meal, but the odd fire-rocket still continued to soar into the sky, lighting up the surface of the lake and the lonely Villa Coralo standing on its farther shore. Behind its dark screen of ilex it looked curiously remote, guarding a secret of its own.

'Tomorrow I will take you back to Rome,' said Tarquin, 'and we will look for your artist together.'

He did not return her portrait, but perhaps he had decided to keep the sketch for further reference, after all. If the initials really were C.S.L. then there could be hope.

They reached the shop by midday, driving through the chaotic traffic of the bright morning at a pace which allowed Harriet to scan the faces of passers-by on the pavement, looking for someone who might be Carlo much as Emmy had done for the past few disheartening weeks. It was like searching for a needle in the proverbial haystack, she thought, as one bearded figure after another passed them by. Strange how many beards there were in Rome when you came to count them, she mused, and not all of them bound for the Piazza di Spagna. Some turned into office buildings, while others vanished into the doorways of shops, none of them remotely resembling the man they sought.

'We'll try again tomorrow,' said Tarquin. 'Meanwhile, I must go to Florence. I have business to do there for my grandmother.'

No doubt he would try to pick up a thread or two there, too. It was a tremendous task he had undertaken in the name of friendship, especially as he seemed determined not to call in the assistance of the police. Not at present, anyway. He was trying to spare Emmy and his grandmother from the renewed curiosity of the gossips, and this she could understand.

Any spare time she had after that was spent in the Piazza di Spagna or the nearby Via Margutta where so many artists had their studios, although sometimes she thought this would be the very last place to find her bearded friend. A studio cost money and he did not appear to have any. Nor did he seem to have an ordered way of life, roving from city to city as the spirit moved him or a commission came his way.

It was a tiring quest with no great hope of reward at the end of it, but she stuck determinedly to the task, climbing the two-hundred-year-old steps again and again until she felt that she knew all one hundred and thirty-seven of them and all the artists and sellers of junk who made a precarious living there. Artists there were in plenty, but none of them turned out to be her bearded friend. It was as if he had vanished completely from the face of the earth.

Once Graziana joined her at the shop and they walked back to the flat together, lingering beside the Bernini fountain where half of Rome seemed to be cooling themselves and gossiping in the last rays of the sun.

'You seem to be prowling around a lot these days,' Graziana observed. 'Is anything wrong?'

Harriet hesitated.

'I was looking for the artist who drew my portrait,' she confessed, not quite sure whether or not she should confide in her companion.

'Why was that?' Graziana asked. 'Were you thinking of offering him another commission? He drew you very well in so short a time, but these types never stay in one place for long. They're birds of passage, as a rule, always on the lookout for something new.'

'I suppose so,' Harriet agreed. 'If you stumbled across him you would let me know?'

'If it means so much to you.'

'It does.'

Graziana gave her a sharp look, although she didn't pursue the subject of itinerant artists in general and Harriet's bearded friend in particular.

Then, one evening, while they were strolling idly through the Pincio to have supper at the Casina Valadier because they were both in funds and it was too hot to cook for themselves in the flat, they experienced the same odd sense of being followed at a distance which Graziana had first remarked on outside the Auditorium.

'That man!' she exclaimed, turning quickly. 'Do you know him?'

Harriet looked round in time to see a tall, bearded figure hurrying away through the crowd of strolling Romans making for the vantage-point of Piazzale del Pincio where they could watch the sun go down. Without thought, and with no proof that she was even remotely on the right trail, she turned away from the crowded terrace, running in the opposite direction in pursuit of the hurrying figure, but as she backed off the Piazzale a group of schoolchildren surged between her and her quarry, completely obscuring her view. When they had passed on their noisy way the bearded figure had disappeared, lost to her in one or other of the tree-shaded lanes which stretched down to the Fountain of Moses and the Water Clock.

Frustrated, she waited for Graziana to join her.

'What was all that about?' the younger girl wanted to know. 'It's decidedly bad form to run after a man, you know!'

'I'm almost sure it was my artist,' Harriet declared.

'Well,' Graziana pointed out, 'you can always try again, because it proves he's still in Rome. Meanwhile, when do we eat?'

They made their way to the Casina, sitting out on the balcony with the swallows darting above their heads and looking down at the whole of Rome spread out before them.

'It's a big city,' Graziana mused. 'Too big to find just one man in a crowd.'

Yet that was what she had set out to do, Harriet thought. To search and search until she found the bearded stranger who might or might not be Carlo Luciano and Emmy's missing husband.

The days of her continuing quest passed quickly enough because Rome seemed busier than ever and now and then Emmy came to the shop, offering to help. On the first occasion they spoke briefly of the artist who had sketched Harriet's portrait.

'I took so little interest in what Carlo did when we were first married,' Emmy confessed. 'I knew he could paint, but I was too taken up with my own affairs and ambitions to think of his. I've looked at your portrait over and over again, but I can't be convinced. The initials are the same, if they really are C.S.L., but that isn't absolute proof, is it?' She bit her lip. 'I'm no real help to Tarquin, behaving like this,' she added, 'but I think that Carlo is dead.' She twisted her delicate-looking hands together in a gesture of despair. 'I wish I knew. Harriet, can you understand how awful it is for me, not knowing?'

'I think I can.' Harriet put a comforting hand on her arm. 'But you just can't give up like that. We've got to go on trying till we are absolutely sure.'

'Tarquin is spending so much time away from the estate hoping to find Carlo,' Emmy said heavily, 'and I don't seem to be helping him very much. I've told him we should go to the police with the information we have and let them sort it out, but for the moment he refuses to listen.' She drew in a long, quivering breath. 'I used to think my life was perfect, my shallow, self-indulgent silly little life which really meant nothing. I thought I had everything I could ever want, but we get back only what we sow, I think. I put nothing into life except vanity and pride, so now I have nothing in return.'

It was a mood which perhaps only Tarquin could deal with effectively and all Harriet could offer at the moment was sympathy.

Then, one morning, when she was replacing a piece of unsold silver in the window, she saw the man she had been looking for. They came face to face as he gazed through the glass and she saw the startled expression in his eyes as he turned hastily away.

In seconds she had reached the pavement outside the shop, darting along the busy thoroughfare in pursuit. He turned a corner and she followed him into the lane where the carriers delivered their goods to the shops.

'Carlo!'

He turned immediately, halting on the cobblestones to look at her.

'You drew my portrait—remember?' She was breathing heavily.

'Yes,' he said without expression. 'Almost three weeks ago.'

'You remember me?'

'Of course. You were Angelo's friend. I knew that you worked at the shop.'

'Is that why you came?'

'Partly.' He gave her an odd, unconvincing smile.

'Please, Carlo,' she begged, 'can we talk? Can we go somewhere and talk for a moment? I have so much to say to you.'

He smiled briefly, an odd, disparaging smile which wrenched at her heart and did not reach to his eyes.

'Not here,' he said. 'It is much too fashionable.'

'Would you come back to the shop?'

He shook his head.

Strange how she could not think of anywhere to go now that she had finally contacted him! His shabby state had nothing to do with it, although he thought it had.

'Can we walk, then, or sit in the sun?'

'We can walk,' he said.

They went up the Via Condotti and across the Piazza, climbing slowly up the familiar Steps.

'I've been coming here a lot these past two weeks, hoping to find you,' she confessed.

'Do you wish me to give you your money back?' he asked with a hint of humour, 'because you do not like your portrait?'

'Nothing like that,' she assured him. 'I want to talk about Emmy.'

He stiffened perceptibly.

'I don't think that would do any good,' he said.

Half way up the Steps he sat down on the sun-warmed

stone as if he could no longer make the effort to reach the top. It was then that she saw how thin he was, his cheeks hollowed under the straggling beard, his eyes sunk deep in their sockets beneath the fine, dark brows.

'You've been ill,' she said, sitting down beside him. 'That's why I haven't been able to find you.'

'It was nothing.' He brushed her concern aside. 'A germ of some sort I picked up in Florence.'

'Were you in hospital?'

He hesitated.

'For a few days. I am well now, as you can see.'

She thought that he looked anything but well as the haunted eyes gazed back steadily into her own.

'Carlo, why don't you get in touch with Tarquin?' she suggested. 'He knows you are alive and somewhere in the vicinity. You've been ill and you can't continue to live like this.'

'Tarquin has done enough.' He smiled faintly. 'He has been a good friend, paying off my debts. It is impossible for me to ask more of him.'

'He doesn't look at it that way,' she answered with absolute conviction. 'He wants you to come home.'

The last word almost unnerved him. She could see the pulse hammering in his cheek and the tight grip of his hand on the edge of the step where they sat.

'I can't,' he said. 'Surely you can see how impossible it is. I made this awful decision. I ran away from my problems like a coward when I had the chance. I thought there was nothing else left for me to do. I thought Emmy wanted her freedom more than anything else. It was a wrong decision. I know that now, but I was desperate, and since then the situation has gone from bad to worse, I haven't made good, as I swore I would. I have nothing to offer Emmy. Nothing at all.'

'Are you still in love with her?' Harriet asked gently.

He looked down towards the busy square where all Rome seemed to be hurrying by.

'What difference would that make?' he asked.

'All the difference in the world.'

He shook his head.

'Failure is all I have to offer her.'

'If she loves you, Carlo, that won't matter at all.'

'How could she love me after what I did?' he protested, his mouth firming again. 'I can't believe that my life will ever come together after this.'

'Give it a chance,' she urged. 'If you can't see Emmy, go and talk to Tarquin.'

He looked down at his hands.

'I can't make any promises,' he said. 'Not now. I've sunk pretty low, as you can see, and Emmy was never keen on drop-outs.'

'You're ill,' she said. 'Let Tarquin take care of you.'

'He's done enough.'

'Oh, Carlo, give him a chance,' she begged. 'He'll go on searching till he finds you, and he has so much to do on the estate. The Contessa has had an accident and he has just brought her back from Capri. Really, he has his hands full.'

'Where is Emmy?' he asked half-heartedly.

'In Rome. Will you go to see her?'

He shook his head.

'I can't plead any more. I did my share of that at Amalfi and she would not listen.'

'Don't blame her too much,' Harriet begged. 'She could have changed, you know. Honestly, I believe she has changed. She's a different person. Why don't you see her and find out for yourself?'

'I can't.' He was adamant. 'It's kind of you to try, but I don't think this can be patched up. I can hardly present myself to her in this state and say: "Please take me back". Surely you can understand this?'

'All I can see is that you need her help and I think she needs you,' Harriet answered. 'She has cut herself off from everybody she used to know and she is very much alone, except for Tarquin.'

'And you? Are you her friend, Harriet? I hope you are,'

he added without waiting for her answer, 'because she must need friends just now.'

'Don't you think she might also need you?' Harriet asked.

He shook his head.

'No way.' There was a harder edge to his voice now. 'I have nothing to offer her. I'm sick, I'm a failure, and I have no real future ahead of me.'

She jumped to her feet.

'As I see it, you're being far too sorry for yourself!' she exclaimed impatiently. 'You're a wonderful artist; you have a talent which you surely must recognise when you can command commissions in a place like Florence. You've been sick, possibly because you have neglected yourself, but really you have a lot going for you. If you give her half a chance, Emmy will look after you.'

He got up to stand beside her, leaning on the stone balustrade as if for support.

'She never liked burdens, and I couldn't thrust this one on her,' he said. 'You know that, Harriet.'

'You could give her the chance to refuse.'

'Perhaps I could,' he said, preparing to move on, 'but I could never go back to Amalfi till Emmy herself asked me to go. She has sold the house and is living elsewhere.'

At least he knew what was happening, and he had been back to Amalfi where Emmy and he had once been happy.

'Think about it,' she said. 'Please give it a second thought.'

As he walked away she wondered if she had proved so eloquent because she had been more or less pleading for her own chance of happiness, but how foolish that might be when Tarquin had never spoken a word of love to her!

CHAPTER SEVEN

WHEN she made her way back to the shop Tarquin was already there.

'Can I speak to you?' she asked. 'Something has just turned up. Something urgent.'

He looked at her wind-blown hair and the bright flush on her cheeks.

'We'll take a cab,' he said, glancing at his watch. 'It's almost lunch time.'

'Give me a minute to tidy up.'

He was waiting in the shop when she parted the curtains again, a taxi already at the curb, and to her surprise he gave the driver an address in the Trastevere.

'We can talk on the way,' he said, 'and I think you deserve a reasonable meal. You look very thin.'

'I keep busy,' she said, not knowing how to begin to tell him about Carlo, 'and it's been very hot in Rome these past few days.'

'We must remedy that with some good hill air,' he suggested. 'My grandmother thought you might like to come to the villa at the weekend. She wants a finger in the pie!'

'She's bound to be interested in what's going on at the shop,' Harriet agreed, the colour deepening in her cheeks at the thought of another visit to the Villa Ilena. 'It's very kind of her to ask me.'

'The truth might be that she is bored with her own company,' he smiled. 'She's as full of energy as ever she was and she wants to be back in the swim as quickly as possible.'

Harriet caught her breath, wondering if it meant that her time in Rome was coming to an end.

'What happened?' he asked abruptly.

'I've seen Carlo.'

140

He turned towards her, all the amusement dying out of his eyes.

'Where?'

'He came to the shop. He was looking in at the window when I went to replace some silver. Tarquin, he's been ill. He's still very sick, but he won't hear of coming back. I think it's because he hasn't made good,' she rushed on when he remained silent. 'I told him that you were searching for him, but he just kept repeating that he was a failure and nobody could possibly want to know.'

'He meant Emmy, of course.' Tarquin's mouth took on a harder line. 'Did you try to persuade him?'

'I did my best. I said you were concerned about him.' She hesitated, looking out at the passing traffic as they drove across the Tiber. 'I also said that I thought Emmy had changed, but I don't think he believed me. He was so utterly obsessed with his own unworthiness—his ultimate failure.'

'He must be feeling very low.' Tarquin gazed down at the yellow river without seeming to notice it. 'What do you think is wrong with him, apart from utter depression?'

'He has neglected his health, and he regrets what he did. Tarquin, he's ashamed, and that's what makes it so pitiful.' She held her breath for a moment. 'He did all he could for Emmy, but it just wasn't enough at the time. Now he feels it's not much use trying any more.'

His gesture of impatience was somehow typical.

'That's no answer,' he said harshly. 'Killing himself in another way isn't going to solve anything.'

'He asked me if I understood and I said I thought I did,' she confessed as they left the river behind and wound through a maze of busy streets honeycombed with narrow passages and studded with little squares where the sun poured down and deep shadows lay along the walls. 'I felt that I couldn't get through to him this time, although there seemed to be some kind of bond between us when he sketched my portrait. I'm sorry, Tarquin,' she apologised. 'I did my best.'

He did not seem to hear her as the taxi pulled up to the curb and the driver jumped out to open the door for them, but when they were finally settled at a secluded table in the cellarlike restaurant he turned to look at her.

'Did he give you an address?' he asked.

She shook her head.

'I doubt if he has one, at least, not permanently,' she said. 'I think he may be just drifting from one place to the next. Rome today, Perugia or Florence by the weekend.'

'Florence?' he mused. 'I think I could find him there. We have a mutual friend. But then we come up against Carlo's infernal pride. He would not ask for anyone's pity. He'd rather die.'

'I tried to explain to him how Emmy felt. How I think she feels,' Harriet amended. 'I said it wouldn't matter how poor he was or what he had done if she loved him.'

'You surprise me,' he said sharply, 'but perhaps you do not practise what you preach.'

'I try to be honest,' she said quietly.

'Then why did you leave Amalfi in such a hurry and go off to London without a word?' he demanded.

She could not tell him that she had been already in love with him then, as she was now, because the harsh change in him seemed to be complete.

'Sometimes we do things against the dictates of our hearts,' she said. 'I was needed in London at the time because my mother was ill and I had no real place here. I explained to the Contessa and she thought it best that I should go. But I've told you all this before and it can't possibly make a difference now.'

He did not contradict her as the waiter approached with their menus.

'I'm not very hungry,' she said.

'Try some fish,' he advised. 'It's always good here.'

When their order was brought he returned to the subject of Carlo without apology.

'I don't think it's going to do much good to tell Emmy that we've drawn a blank,' he said, frowning. 'I'd rather have something more definite to suggest. I'll stay in Rome for a couple of days, looking around, and then I'll drive you out to the villa.'

'I could quite easily find my own way,' she offered. 'Or Angelo might be persuaded to take me.'

'He wouldn't need much persuasion,' he returned dryly, 'but it might be a good thing if he went home more often. I've told my grandmother that Carlo isn't dead, by the way, so you needn't feel that you have to pretend more than is absolutely necessary.'

'I'm glad she knows,' said Harriet. 'She's not the sort of person who would be easily hoodwinked.'

'You know her very well!' He turned the conversation away from Carlo and Emmy. 'I hope Angelo isn't going to make things too difficult.'

'In what way?'

'Kicking over the traces again, as he did once before.'

'Perhaps he's older and wiser now.'

'You have a great faith in people, Harriet!'

'Why not? I think everyone should be given the benefit of the doubt. Angelo is bright and attractive and—loving in his way, and he's very fond of his family. He also values your advice, though you might not think so,' she added. 'Give him a chance to prove that he really cares about the estate and I don't think you'll be disappointed.'

'You are a clever advocate,' he said briefly. 'I hope Angelo appreciates your concern.'

A hot colour suffused her cheeks.

'You're far too hard on him,' she declared. 'He did come home, after all. He *is* trying!'

'We will not argue,' he said. 'I hope that he will not disappoint my grandmother a second time.'

She knew how closely knit Roman families were and how much the Contessa longed to see her grandsons united on the estate, and now she knew that it was also Tarquin's wish.

'He won't go away,' she said. 'I feel sure. Not unless

something dramatic was to happen, and even then I think you could reason with him.'

He smiled at the thought as their plates were cleared away.

'What now?' he asked lightly, as if their conversation had been entirely trivial.

'Nothing more, thank you.' She put her napkin aside. 'I really must get back to the shop as early as possible. It's such a busy day.'

'Do you want Emmy to help in the morning?' he asked.

She ran her tongue along her upper lip because it suddenly felt dry.

'If you see her you can ask her to come.'

It was still Emmy; Emmy always there, standing between them. But if Emmy really meant what she said, if she wanted to take Carlo back, Tarquin would be alone.

When they finally reached the shop it was full of customers.

'Will you come in?' she asked as he helped her out of the taxi. 'I could make you some tea.'

'It's a temptation, but I have work to do,' he explained. 'I mean to go on with the search, Harriet,' he added, 'so if you are able to help in any way will you let me know?'

'Immediately,' she promised. 'And thanks for the lunch. It was a change from *spaghetti alla matriciana* or just plain bread and *pecorino*, which is Dino's favourite!'

A change and so much more, yet her wretched pride would not let him see how much it had meant to her.

Angelo was haggling with a would-be customer when she went in.

'*Ecco la* Signorina Voyle!' he announced thankfully. 'She will explain how much value you have there, and then perhaps you will believe me that the price is not ridiculous!'

The abashed young man set the silver ornament down on the glass-topped showcase, backing away from it reluctantly.

'Can I help you?' Harriet asked. 'The price is too much, perhaps? In that case, would you like to look at something else? This, for instance, which is similar although it is smaller in size.' She picked up a delicately-carved bonbon dish which, in her own opinion, was much superior in design. 'You will see how beautifully it is made.'

When the young man had gone happily on his way clutching the pretty little dish she turned to Angelo.

'That was disgraceful of you, trying to browbeat the poor young man into buying something he couldn't really afford,' she declared.

'Dino would call it salesmanship!' Angelo protested. 'Anyway, what would you call your persuasive charm?'

'Common sense,' she told him promptly on her way through the curtains. 'A satisfied customer who believes he has been given good advice and obtained a bargain is much better than a disgruntled one who has paid too much and will never come in again.'

'What has Tarquin been saying to upset you?' he asked, following her into the inner room. 'You looked distinctly peeved as you said goodbye.'

'He gave me lunch.' She hesitated. 'We'd been talking about Emmy.'

'Ah!' he said. 'A thorny subject, to be sure! Once he tore a strip off me for pretending to be in love with Emmy, but here in Rome such affairs are not taken too seriously unless there is a scandal lurking in the background. Only people like Tarquin and my grandmother are perturbed by them.'

'You've never been truly in love,' Harriet said. 'Otherwise you couldn't think that way.'

'Maybe I will change as I grow older,' he smiled. 'You could teach me how.'

'No!' she said sharply. 'You're no more in love with me than you were with Emmy. Your values are all wrong, but I think you know that already.'

He looked nonplussed for a moment.

'Tell me,' he said, 'why you avoid Tarquin whenever you can.'

She remained silent.

'Not because you are in love with him, surely? Oh, Harri, I think you are! I have stumbled on your secret,' he declared, 'and I am sorry—truly sorry for you, because my brother is a determined man. He will not marry until he can be sure there will be no mistake, like the mistake Carlo made, and he would not ask anyone to share his life until all the rumours about Carlo's disappearance had been quashed. Then he can take a wife with honour. My grandmother thinks in the same way, although she is now impatient to see a new generation of de Filippos at Cerano.'

'You would please her very much if you married and settled down, Angelo,' Harriet suggested to hide her own embarrassment. 'Surely there's someone——'

'Someone!' he laughed. 'There is always "someone", my dear Harri! Don't you know that I am the eternal Lothario, the gay Don Juan who can never make a decision about love until it is too late? You see in me not a reflection of my worthy brother, but the replica of the Conte Niccolo, who was my grandfather and a very gay young man indeed!'

'He made the Contessa very happy,' Harriet pointed out.

'Ah, yes, that is very true, but I understand that he was thirty before they married. The age of discretion, would you think?'

'I think it's time we got back to work,' Harriet answered dryly. 'Emmy may be in tomorrow, by the way, to wrap parcels.'

In the morning, however, Emmy did not make her expected appearance, and Harriet supposed that something more important than sealing their gift-wrapped parcels with bright green wax had cropped up to detain her. It might have been the fact that Tarquin had traced Carlo, at last, and they were talking about the future.

The day seemed very long, although the shop remained as busy as usual, and by closing time Harriet had ceased to look up with a rapidly-beating heart each time the door opened. Trying not to jump to her feet each time the telephone bell shrilled through the flat, she spent a quiet evening alone with Graziana.

'The Contessa wants me to go to the villa tomorrow,' she said as she prepared the supper. 'Will you come?'

'Sorry, I can't! I'm going out with an old friend.'

Graziana seemed so pleased about her invitation that Harriet was almost tempted to ask if the 'old friend' was Angelo.

'You don't know him,' Graziana assured her, as if she had read her thoughts. 'He's an American. I met him the other day in the Corso and he's here for a month. I didn't get to see him last time he was in Rome, so we're kind of making up for it. How will you get to the villa?' she asked absently.

Harriet hesitated.

'Tarquin half promised to take me.'

'What do you mean "half"? He's either going to take you or he's not.' Graziana eyed her speculatively. 'What's happening, for goodness' sake?'

'He's—worried about Emmy. Graz,' Harriet confessed, 'I met Carlo the other day. He's in Rome.'

Graziana stared back at her in bewilderment.

'You *met* him? Then it's true. He didn't drown that day, after all! The police have thought it all along. That's why they put his name on the missing persons list. You didn't know that, perhaps?'

'Tarquin told me.'

'Does Angelo know about Carlo?' Graziana demanded, frowning.

'I'm not sure, but I think Tarquin will tell him in time.'

'In time!' Graziana cried. 'He ought to know *now*. He has suffered enough, believing himself responsible for the accident although it was Tarquin who took the blame. Angelo knows how foolish he was and he's truly sorry, I guess. Sometimes I get all het up about how he behaves, but I know he's honest enough deep down. It's just that he loves life and he's full of exuberance. We can't blame him for that!'

She took up the guitar Angelo had given her, strumming thoughtfully as Harriet carried a tray to the window where they could enjoy the faint breeze coming from the Borghese gardens.

'Why are you going to Cerano?' she asked.

'The Contessa wants to talk shop.' Harriet set down the tray. 'Her health is greatly improved and Tarquin says she wants to have a finger in the pie again.'

'She sure will, but I think there might be something else she wants to know.' Graziana struck a final chord. 'She's an outrageous schemer, you know, especially where the family is concerned. I reckon she has our futures all mapped out for us and, in the end, there won't be a thing we can do about it.'

'She's very conscious of keeping you together as a family.'

Graziana nooded.

'It's the old Roman tradition dying hard in her case,' she reflected. 'Grandparents as well as parents had a big say in their children's destinies at one time, and the Contessa is a very proud Roman matron. She reminds me of the mother of the Gracchi, tall and stately as a mountain pine, but with a will of iron where her family is concerned.'

'Don't frighten me too much!' Harriet laughed. 'I may have to give an account of myself tomorrow.'

The idea had been in her mind for some time. The shop had been doing well, but the fact that Angelo was not taking an interest in the silver trade might make a difference to his grandmother should she decide to return to Rome herself to take over. Harriet had been doing a certain amount of buying, but she knew that it would be a long time before she acquired the full knowledge she needed, and certainly she would never be able to replace Renata de Filippo in the auction marts. The Contessa had the finesse of long experience and knowledge, which she believed she would never possess, and at times she had thought of herself merely as a stopgap, waiting to be dismissed when her services were no longer needed.

Well, she had known all that when she had agreed to return to Rome, and now she might be coming very near to the end of her usefulness. Of course, the Contessa would concern herself with her family first.

During the morning, when the shop was even busier than usual, she tried not to look up each time the street door opened, and it was late afternoon before Tarquin put in an appearance. He looked tired, as if he had just come off a long journey, and his mouth was grim.

'Ready?' he asked briefly.

She had packed a weekend bag the evening before, taking as little as possible with her in case she might have to make the journey to the Villa Ilena by bus, but seemingly Tarquin kept his promises even though he had not managed to confirm them in the meantime. A telephone message had come through from the Contessa to say that she was expecting them late that evening, but that was all.

'Have you anything to report?' she asked under her breath, knowing that he had been searching for Carlo.

'Nothing.' He lifted her grip. 'Is this all you have?'

'I thought I should travel light in case I had to fight my way on to a bus!'

'You knew I would pick you up. I said so.'

'Yes, I'm sorry. I should have realised that.' She followed him to the door. 'Angelo will lock up.'

'He's not coming with us?'

'I don't think so. He has—something else to do.'

'And Graziana?'

'She's meeting an old friend—an American who is in Rome on business.'

Tarquin frowned, but she didn't think he was unduly perturbed about his cousin. He had other things on his mind.

His car was parked at the curb with a sense of shock Harriet realised that Emmy was sitting in the front passenger seat. She, too, was going to the Villa Ilena. Had Tarquin insisted on her being invited or had the summons come from the Contessa herself?

There was no opportunity to reason out an answer as Tarquin held open the rear door for her to get in and

Emmy offered her a quivering smile. She was so obviously near to tears that Harriet could not bring herself to ask about Carlo.

It was a glorious evening for a drive up into the foothills of the mountains through typical little towns topped by a castle and past ancient monasteries looking down serenely on the vineyards at their feet. Little churches which were gems of Byzantine construction slipped past, dominating the villages they served, and at almost every cottage door old women sat on kitchen chairs, gossiping in the last of the sun. Little boys, as strong as the infant Hercules, played in the fountains while their more timid sisters stood at the edge watching the fun.

Amid the ruins of a *palazzo* nature had spilled a treasure-trove of flowering vines toppling from marble urns and over broken walls to dazzle the eye and add to the impression that the past was still alive here, marching hand-in-hand with the present.

Two Little Sisters of the Poor stood by the roadside as they passed. Like all nuns, they were very jolly, waving a greeting when Emmy smiled to them, and Tarquin pulled up to ask if he might drop them at their destination. Eagerly they climbed into the back of the car beside Harriet, chattering in voluble Italian without really expecting an answer, and when they got out at the next village they expressed their thanks with a simple blessing which touched Emmy so much that she turned her head away to hide her sudden tears.

'We have no news,' Tarquin said then. 'We have searched most of Rome in the past two days and have come up with nothing but disappointment.'

He had been looking for Carlo all that time, and Emmy had been with him, hoping to contact her husband in vain.

They reached the estate as the sun went down, painting the sky beyond the vineyards in apricot and gold. Tiny clouds trailed along the horizon in bands of white tinged by the afterglow, and the villa itself had taken on a warm, rosy glow in the half-light. The silver-grey olive trees, the cypresses and ilex standing out against the softening evening sky spoke of a peace and protection which had lasted for hundreds of years, here in this place, and the Contessa standing on the terrace steps to welcome them was part of it. She was no longer leaning on the ebony stick she had depended on at Anacapri, although she limped a little as she walked towards them.

'I hope you have had a pleasant drive from Rome,' she said as they got out. 'I think you will now be hungry, so we will dine a little early this evening. Tarquin, I have managed very well in your absence, you will be pleased to know,' she added. 'I have sold a great deal of wine!'

Tarquin kissed her on both cheeks.

'So long as it was the right vintage!' he smiled, the traces of fatigue erased from his eyes for a moment. 'Is there really nothing you cannot do, Nonna?'

'Many things,' she admitted as she turned to Harriet. 'We have much work to do together,' she announced. 'I have had a dealer here all afternoon and finally I have bought a good many things I may speedily regret.'

Tarquin drew Emmy forward.

'There is still no news,' he said to his grandmother in much the same tone he had used to Harriet.

'Thank you for letting me come with Tarquin,' Emmy said in a small, subdued voice. 'It is very good of you.'

Renata de Filippo looked at her with pity in her eyes.

'You must want to go to your room immediately,' she said not unkindly, although there was a hint of reserve in her quiet voice. 'I will have a meal sent up to you, if you wish.'

'You are most kind,' said Emmy, 'but I can't put you to so much trouble. I am not ill, only tired. One does not sleep very well in Rome.'

The Contessa led the way indoors.

'Tarquin will pour you some wine,' she said. 'Perhaps, after you have changed, you will feel better.'

She was being the thoughtful hostess and Emmy acknowledged the effort she had made by proffering the gift she had brought with her from the Via Condotti.

'It's something I thought you might like,' she said almost shyly, 'although you already have so many beautiful things.'

The Contessa put the gift aside to accept Harriet's gift of flowers.

'They are beautiful,' said Renata. 'I will arrange them in my own room.'

Emmy did come down for supper, after all, dressed simply in blue. It was a colour which suited her even more than the pink silk had done, giving her an ethereal look which was emphasised by her deeply-shadowed eyes. Harriet smoothed the folds of her printed cotton with an odd sense of inferiority. No one could look like Emmy did now and fail to command sympathy and respect.

Tarquin rose to draw a chair forward for her. The windows leading on to the terrace were wide open, but the table had been set in the room itself because the night air would soon turn cold. They spoke of Rome as he poured their wine from a lovely silver jug which had been finely chased by a master hand several hundred years ago, perhaps on this very spot. The wine, Harriet noticed, was always their own, poured with a suggestion of pride in achievement which seemed perfectly natural in this place where de Filippos had lived and loved and died for centuries.

When the meal was over Emmy excused herself immediately.

'I feel really tired now,' she confessed. 'If you don't mind, I would like to go to my room.'

Tarquin walked with her to the foot of the staircase.

'Perhaps, if you are not too tired, we could take a look at the things I have just bought,' the Contessa suggested. 'It will not take long, and tomorrow you will wish to ride out with Tarquin when he makes his rounds of the estate.'

Her heart beating faster than it should have done, Harriet followed her from the room in time to see Tarquin placing a protective arm about Emmy's shoulders. He bent his head to kiss her on the cheek, but Emmy reached up to throw her arms about his neck.

'Oh, Tarquin! Tarquin!' she cried. 'What is going to happen now?'

Before they could hear his answer the Contessa had led the way in the opposite direction, towards the library, switching on the lights as they entered the long, book-lined room where her recent purchases were laid out on the massive walnut table which graced the centre of the floor.

'See what you think,' she asked, slightly tight-lipped as she watched her grandson go out at the big main door. 'Take your time to examine them. I will tidy up the wrappings while I wait.'

She had made no reference to Emmy and Harriet turned to the array of articles on the table wondering what the outcome of this strange weekend would be.

The silver miniatures had been selected with care and attention to detail and there was no doubt that the Contessa had bought well.

'They are just right,' she said at the end of her examination. 'If I were you I wouldn't be able to part with some of them.'

'Then you would be a poor businesswoman,' Renata told her with an indulgent smile. 'It is folly to be too senti-mental, even with the most precious things. Yes, they are all very beautiful,' she agreed, lifting a delicate tortoiseshell box to hold it to the light, 'but we must not keep such beauty entirely for ourselves. We must share it and take a joy from the fact that others can also appreciate it.' She gazed down at Harriet's busy hands. 'You do not wear a ring of any kind,' she remarked. 'Why is that?'

'I'm—not very fond of them,' Harriet confessed, 'unless they mean something.'

The Contessa smiled.

'You prefer a necklace,' she suggested. 'What have you done with the pretty cameos you wore so much in Capri?'

A deep wave of embarrassment coloured Harriet's cheeks.

'I gave it back.' Her voice sounded strangled. 'It was a present, but I gave it back.'

'A love gift, perhaps?'

'No—it wasn't that.'

'Such a pity,' Renata sighed. 'It looked so beautiful and it must have been quite valuable.'

'Yes.'

They were standing looking down at the table when Tarquin came in.

'Quite a bit of loot!' he observed, turning the tortoiseshell box over in his hand. 'Do you want us to take it all back to Rome?'

'It would be a good idea,' his grandmother said almost impatiently. 'I have gathered enough here in my lifetime to furnish many homes. It can become a disease, in the end, if we are not firm with ourselves in the beginning.'

They wandered back to the little *sala*.

'In the morning,' said Renata, 'you must take Harriet with you to ride round the estate. It is time she had some good hill air in her lungs after all these dreadful petrol fumes one has to breathe in Rome.'

CHAPTER EIGHT

THE morning dawned fresh and cool. Harriet had borrowed Graziana's cream riding-breeches, wearing them with a cinnamon-coloured shirt and brown boots, and from somewhere Tarquin had produced a riding-hat which fitted her. She stuffed her hair into it, preparing to get into the saddle by herself, but he was by her side in an instant.

'Don't tempt fate!' he said in the bantering tone he sometimes used. 'It's much too early in the morning to bite the dust!'

'It's the most beautiful morning I've ever seen,' she decided extravagantly. 'Do you ride out as early as this every day?'

He nodded, drawing a deep breath as his grey eyes ranged over the nearer foothills to the distant boundary of the estate.

'I'm afraid so. It will take all of three hours to cover everything I want to inspect. I have been away for almost a full week,' he reminded her.

She looked down at her bridle.

'Are you sure I won't hold you up?' she asked, quite prepared to ride alone.

'I have to make scheduled stops along the way,' he explained. 'It's not the sort of job you can rush, especially when everyone wants to talk and the vines are growing well!'

He stooped so that she could put her foot in his hand to vault into the saddle, and she saw how his dark hair grew strongly into the nape of his neck and how taut his brown skin looked beneath the fine silk shirt he wore. Suddenly she swayed towards him, as if the whole world had been blotted out by his tall, lean figure and only the faint light in the sky remained.

He caught her instantly, steadying her on her feet while a small pulse began to hammer in his cheek.

'I'm sorry,' she said. 'I'm not very good with horses.'

She was close enough to hear his sharply indrawn breath as he straightened to his full height.

'You'll learn,' he said, lifting her bodily into the saddle. When she had taken the reins he did not mount immediately.

'We're waiting for Emmy,' he said. 'She insists that she should come with us for the exercise.'

Emmy came on to the terrace as Enrico led another horse round the end of the villa from the direction of the stables.

'A lovely morning!' she declared. 'Far too nice to spend in bed. I'm much better now,' she added for Tarquin's benefit. 'All the cobwebs blown away!'

They rode for over an hour, as the sun strengthened, going up through the terraces where already men were at work among the vines, and finally riding under the olives till they reached the top of a hill. Here the whole vast estate lay beneath them, acre after acre of growing vines interspaced with wine lodges and tiny white-washed dwellings covered in bougainvillea and honeysuckle and backed by the gnarled old trees which had produced their abundant harvest year after year for generation after generation of de Filippos and would do so for generations to come. But after this they would bear the name of Greymont because Tarquin's mother had married an Englishman. Somehow, Harriet thought, they would still be known as the de Filippo plantations, whatever the law might say.

Emmy looked beyond the olive trees towards the lake where the Villa Coralo glistened among the ilex trees.

'It seems so far away,' she said. 'In another world.'

Tarquin turned his horse's head in the opposite direction.

'We'll go down this way,' he said.

With a sigh of regret Harriet followed him, but soon they were galloping over open terrain and she could feel the fresh hill wind in her face and the surge of power in her horse's flanks as he bore her along. The sun was warm on her back and she swept off her hat to let her hair blow free. It was like riding the wind itself, on and on without stopping, on and on with Tarquin by her side.

And Emmy! She turned in the saddle to see Emmy far behind them, a small, forlorn figure, walking her horse at the edge of a ravine.

'We must wait for her,' said Tarquin, reining in the powerful gelding he rode with ease. 'She tires easily.'

Emmy had not wanted to gallop lightheartedly in the face of the wind, and who could blame her? She came up with them at last, murmuring her apologies.

'I've slowed you down,' she said. 'I'm sorry. Perhaps I should not have come.'

'It isn't good for you to sit around all day long,' Tarquin pointed out, 'but you can indulge in a nice long *siesta* now with a clear conscience. I have just one more call to make and then we can return.'

Riding back by a circular route, they visited the last of the wine lodges where a great deal of activity was in progress. Carts stacked high with empty barrels were standing before the open door, waiting their turn to unload while their drivers dozed fitfully in the red dust with their hats pulled down over their eyes. The workers inside the lodge sang at their tasks, filling the dim interior with glorious sound to rival the birds pouring out their hearts in ecstasy among the orchard trees. Flowers, and music, and the glitter of the sun seemed to bound the horizon before it was time to return to the Villa Ilena and the realisation of the future.

The telephone in the hall was ringing as they reached the Villa.

'For you, *signorino*!' Enrico announced, handing the receiver to Tarquin. 'Twice before it has been ringing. Tring! Tring! as if it would never stop!'

Tarquin took the call as they went to change out of their riding breeches.

'You have enjoyed yourself very well,' Emmy suggested

with a faint smile as they reached the top of the staircase. 'Yes, I see that is so,' she added before Harriet could reply.

When they came down again Tarquin was waiting in the hall.

'I have to go to Rome,' he said, looking at Emmy. 'Something has come up.'

'Carlo?' The word was no more than a whisper as Emmy moved towards him. 'I must go with you.' She caught the soft folds of his shirt in her delicate-looking hands. 'I must!'

Tarquin disengaged her fingers from the fine silk.

'No, Emmy,' he said. 'There is no reason for us both to go. This may be no more than another false alarm.'

'How can I stay?' she protested. 'You must take me with you.'

'Emmy,' he begged, 'try to understand. I have nothing definite to go on—yet. As soon as I have I will come for you.'

He went into the little *sala* to speak to his grandmother and Emmy sank down on the nearest chair.

'How can I wait without knowing?' she cried. 'I must see Carlo! I must make him understand.'

Harriet put a comforting hand on her arm.

'Tarquin will keep his promise,' she said. 'He will come back for you.'

They watched him go, driving away along the road and leaving a little cloud of red dust in his wake as the Contessa came out on to the terrace to join them. She looked at Emmy with deep concern in her eyes.

'You will lie down after we have had some lunch,' she suggested. 'It will do you good.'

Harriet, who had never been able to adjust to the *siesta* hour, wandered through the garden when the others went to their separate rooms. It was cool beneath the trees and she had a book to read, but it remained unopened even when she returned to the loggia to sit on one of the marble benches where the shadows gathered in the afternoon. The deep quiet of *siesta* was everywhere, and even the birds had ceased to sing. In the stillness a small green lizard darted across the flags, pausing to gaze at her with bright, inquisitive eyes before it scuttled off along the wall. The Villa Ilena seemed to be deserted.

The workers in the vineyard were also taking their rest so that she seemed the only restless soul in the whole world. Except, perhaps, for Tarquin who had gone in pursuit of the future.

Walking again, she found the path which she had taken with Graziana to the Villa Coralo and presently she found herself standing beside the lake where they had seen Emmy with the little dog. It was now at the Villa Ilena, safe under the Contessa's protective roof.

For a long time she walked beside the water, a kerchief over her head to protect her from the sun. What would Emmy do if Tarquin failed to contact her husband, or even if Carlo should refuse to return? He had been adamant that day when she had followed him from the shop, determined not to thrust himself on Emmy because he had so little to offer her, and all her arguments had proved in vain.

Would Tarquin fare any better if they did meet? Perhaps a man could reason with a man to better effect.

Walking rapidly, she reached the top of the gentle slope which commanded a broad view of the Villa Coralo and the lake with the orchards surrounding it. All the lovely blossom had gone from the orange trees, but they were now in full leaf, like a green sea flowing beside the blue lake, with the exquisite little villa like a gem in their midst. Perhaps Emmy would even go back there one day if Carlo did not return with her to Amalfi.

There were so many ifs and buts, she realised, and no way of seeing into the future for any of them. What was it Angelo had said? That Tarquin would not seek personal happiness until all the rumours about Carlo's disappearance had been quashed, and even then he would not marry until he could be sure that there would be no mistake.

The fact that he might be in love with Emmy could no longer be dismissed. He cared about her and he had treated her with tenderness on more than one occasion, so that Emmy would have been less than human if she had not responded.

Restlessly Harriet walked on without realising how far she had come, but the sun was well down towards the western horizon when she retraced her steps to the Villa Ilena. Tarquin had been in Rome for six hours now, she realised. What had he found?

They had gathered in the small *sala* when they heard the returning car and Emmy jumped nervously to her feet, spilling her wine.

'It's Tarquin!' she exclaimed. 'He has come back——'

It seemed as if she could not move and Tarquin was at the door before any of them could speak. Harriet noticed how grey his face was and how firmly his hands were clenched. Without having to be told, she knew that he had found Carlo.

Swiftly he strode across the room to where Emmy was standing, the half-empty glass still in her hand.

'You've found him,' she said between dry lips. 'Where is he?'

With a quick glance in the Contessa's direction, Tarquin led her to the nearest chair, bending over her with the utmost concern.

'This is going to come as a terrible shock to you, Emmy,' he said quietly. 'It was the police who sent for me. Carlo was found yesterday on the Ponte Cavour——'

'He is dead!' Emmy struggled to her feet again, her lips ashen. 'You have come to tell me that he is dead!'

'No.' Tarquin pressed her back into the chair, his hands gentle as he knelt beside her. 'But he is very ill,' he added slowly. 'He has been ill for some time and he neglected himself shamefully, not wanting to ask for help. They have taken him to hospital and he is being cared for.'

'But they do not think he will live?' The anxious blue eyes searched his, demanding the absolute truth. 'Do not try to spare me, Tarquin. I must know!'

He hesitated only for a moment before he said:

'You know I would never lie to you. He is ill, Emmy— seriously ill. He may not survive the night.'

'Then I must go to him.' Emmy's words were scarcely audible in the quiet room. 'I must go immediately.' She looked about her in a bewildered way, as if she couldn't quite remember where she was. 'Will you take me, Tarquin? Will you come with me for both our sakes?'

Renata de Filippo crossed the room to stand beside her.

'You must go at once,' she said. 'Tarquin will take good care of you.'

Emmy sat quite still, the half-empty glass clenched in her hand.

'Everyone is being so kind,' she said vaguely.

Harriet took the glass from her to set it down on a near-by table.

'Tarquin is waiting,' she said gently. 'I'll get your coat.'

She ran up the marble staircase, searching in the big wardrobe in Emmy's room to find a suitable wrap for the journey to Rome. It would have to be warm because Emmy might have to stay at the hospital all night. Emmy and Tarquin.

Finally she selected a white woollen coat with a hood attached, collecting a stouter pair of shoes on her way out. Emmy had been wearing light sandals in the colour of her dress when she had come down to the *sala* half an hour ago, frail, inadequate things which suggested the Emmy she had come to know.

Kneeling down on the floor in front of her, Harriet took off the satin sandals and slipped her feet into the shoes while Tarquin stood waiting to put the warm coat across her shoulders before they went out. Whatever the coming night might bring, Emmy was once again cocooned in love and affection.

Still kneeling there, Harriet looked at Tarquin, but she could not read his thoughts. He stood above her, tall, distinguished and commanding, tearing her heart to shreds.

'If you are ready,' he said when Emmy raised her eyes to his, 'we will go.'

Harriet remained with the Contessa on the terrace steps as they drove away.

'How ill is he, do you think?' Renata asked. 'I did not meet Carlo very often these past few years, but he seemed to be a robust sort of boy when he came here with Tarquin. Sometimes I could not understand the friendship between them, but it must have been deep,' she added. 'At one time Tarquin was never away from Amalfi, where the Lucianos had their summer villa, and I suppose that was what gave rise to the eventual gossip. *Chi tace confessa!* How true that is, Harriet, for to keep silent is not always wise. Tarquin, of course, has this deep reserve and he will not discuss some things, even with me. He keeps his feelings *in petto* most of the time, and even now I do not know if he will marry Emmy should Carlo die. I think it would be a great pity, of course, but I am too old, and therefore too wise, to tell him so. He is a grown man and he must do with his life as he wishes.' She turned to re-enter the *sala.* '*Che serà, serà,*' she sighed, crossing to the window to look out. 'Do you believe that we cannot do battle with our fate, Harriet?'

'I think there are—some things we can't change, no matter how much we try,' Harriet answered unhappily. 'We wish so hard for what we want, but sometimes it escapes us through no fault of our own. We can't always bend circumstances to our will especially when we're crying for the moon.'

'I do not think you would weep for the impossible,' the Contessa reflected. 'You are much too sensible for that, but on the other hand, it is folly to give up too easily. Do you wish to stay in Rome?'

The question had been at the back of Harriet's mind for some time. Could she bear to stay, meeting Tarquin often and knowing him in love with someone else?

'I must return to London sooner or later,' she said. 'It is my home.'

'You understand, of course, that I could not manage the business without you?' Her employer's words were almost harsh. 'Are you preparing to let me down?'

'I would never do that!' Harriet exclaimed. 'Surely you know that I won't leave till you have someone to put in my place.'

'I am not sufficiently recovered to manage without you, nor am I ready to train a replacement,' Renata said firmly, her shrewd brown eyes fixed on Harriet's. 'If you must go to London periodically to remind yourself that you are an Englishwoman I will send you there to buy for me from time to time. I am tired of that dreary Channel crossing and I will not fly, so what better arrangement could we make?'

'You have Angelo and Graziana now,' Harriet pointed out.

'Angelo—perhaps.' The dark eyes lit up for a moment. 'Of course, I hope that my younger grandson will stay in the land of his birth and finally grow up, but Graziana?' She shrugged her elegant shoulders. 'I think she will go back to America, where perhaps she belongs.'

'Not if you ask her to stay,' said Harriet. 'In some ways she is very Italian.'

'Does she hope to marry Angelo?' Renata asked inquisitively.

'If he asks her I feel sure she will.'

'So!' The Contessa looked satisfied. 'Another link,' she murmured. 'Another harvest gathered in. Harriet, I wish you to marry Tarquin,' she added.

Harriet held her breath.

'But that's impossible!' she managed, at last.

Renata smiled.

'I never use the word,' she declared, 'and neither must you. Tarquin was attracted to you when you first met, I believe.' She held up her hand to silence any protest. 'Do not trouble to deny it, because my eyes are sharp! But he is not a man to hang his heart on his sleeve. He is English in that respect, of course, and you ran off to London before he had a chance to tell you. It made him think you had other fish to fry and you stayed away a long time. Then, of course, there were all the rumours to live down. He let them go because of Angelo. Oh, he thinks I know nothing about him and his reasons for doing so, but I do not like sacrifices. *I* knew what Angelo was up to, and I also knew that Tarquin did not want to see me hurt. Angelo was my *bambino*, you see; my lovely child. He was so fair and beautiful when my daughter first put him into my arms, and when she died so soon afterwards how could I not spoil him? With Tarquin it was different. He was always his father's son, dark and fiercely independent, but he was good for the estate. He would work hard all his life for what he believed in and that is of great importance. Yes,' she mused, 'I knew them both and I knew Angelo's faults. He is like his grandfather, yet Niccolo and I had a happy marriage once I let him see that I wasn't going to stand any nonsense!'

'Graziana would be like that with Angelo,' Harriet decided. 'Even now, she tells him exactly what she thinks.'

'Her mother did also,' the Contessa smiled. 'She told me that she would go to the ends of the earth, let alone America, to marry the man she loved!'

Harriet smiled.

'And she went! I think all your children had very strong personalities,' she suggested.

'Strong in different ways,' Renata acknowledged. 'Sophia and Donna were very much alike. It's a pity that you did not know Tarquin's mother,' she mused. 'She was determined that her sons would grow up to be good Romans, yet she did not want them to forget the English tradition. That, I suppose, was why Tarquin felt drawn to you in the first place.'

'It was a long time ago,' Harriet pointed out, knowing how much Tarquin had changed since then.

'Tch! What are a couple of years in a lifetime?' the Contessa demanded. 'I will speak to Tarquin when he returns.'

'No! Please don't do that,' Harriet implored. 'You see, I went off for no good reason. I—jumped to the wrong conclusion about Emmy, for one thing, and he's aware of it. I was too proud—too easily hurt to stay and have to listen to the rumours.'

'And there was also your mother's health to consider. You should have told Tarquin about that because it was probably your main reason for going as quickly as you did.'

'He knows that now,' said Harriet, picking up the used wine glasses to set them on a tray. 'It hasn't made any difference.'

They dined early, sitting out on the loggia where there was no wind and the scent of honeysuckle and roses drifted in to them from the garden. Emmy's little dog came to sit at the Contessa's feet, mystified by his mistress's abrupt departure.

'They know quite well when something is wrong,' said Renata, fondling his head. 'They are as wise as we are.'

'I'll take him for a walk before I go to bed,' Harriet offered, knowing that she would not sleep easily. 'It's a lovely night.'

It was all so peaceful, so quiet in the villa gardens, yet far away, in Rome, a turmoil of pain and indecision would be raging in Emmy's breast.

'She looks so frail,' she said involuntarily.

'Emmy?' The Contessa gave the suggestion a moment's thought. 'Yes, she does, but those frail-looking ones often survive a catastrophe better than most. As far as I know, she has never been ill in her life. She was greatly pampered by an indulgent father after her mother died, but the man married for a second time—a much younger woman than himself, I understand.'

'Emmy told me,' said Harriet. 'She didn't get on with her stepmother.'

Renata laughed.

'That's an understatement, my dear!' she said. 'Their frequent quarrelling was the talk of Rome at one time. Yes,' she reflected, 'Emmy was always in the limelight in one way or another.' She put her table napkin aside. 'I am surprised there is no word from Tarquin,' she observed, glancing at the fob-watch pinned to the lace of her dress. 'A telephone call, perhaps.' She moved towards the *sala* door. 'If it wasn't for this wretched leg of mine I would walk with you, but it gets painful in the evening if I've been standing a lot during the day. I'll wait for you in here,' she decided, 'in case there should be a call from Rome. Don't walk too far, and don't you think you should take a wrap of some kind? The evenings can be very chilly.'

Harriet took up the woollen shawl she had brought down from her bedroom.

'This will do,' she said. 'I won't go far.'

Calling the dog, she went out across the loggia into the shadowed garden beyond where a nightingale was singing among the trees. She could not believe that all this beauty might be lost to her in a very short time, but the fact remained that she could not stay in Rome for ever. When the Contessa was well enough to manage the shop on her own again, she must go.

Her heart contracted at the thought and she could not imagine what the future might hold for her when she went away.

'Come on, Sergio!' she called to the dog. 'Time to go home!'

The word tugged at her heart as she retraced her steps along the kerb-bordered pathway. The Villa Ilena shining among the tall ilex trees ahead of her would be 'home' to Tarquin for the rest of his lfe.

'No news,' the Contessa announced when she made her appearance at the *sala* door. 'Perhaps they will not phone, after all. I would have thought——'

The telephone bell shrilled through the empty hall before she had finished her sentence.

'Will you take it?' she asked.

Harriet's heart began to beat more quickly as she lifted the receiver. No one but Tarquin would phone them so late as this.

'Is that you, Harriet?' His voice came, sharp and insistent, across the line.

'Yes. I have just come in from the garden. Tarquin, have you any news? Do you want me to call the Contessa?'

'No. I hoped you would answer the phone. There's no need to disturb her. I wanted to talk to you.'

'Carlo?' she asked.

'He is much the same. I think you gathered that he was very ill indeed.'

'Yes.'

'I want you to come to Rome.'

She bit her lip.

'I don't think I could get there tonight.'

'Tomorrow,' he said. 'That will do. I will send a car for you in the morning. I'm sorry about this, spoiling your weekend, but Emmy needs your help. It appears that you're the only one she can talk to just now.'

'I feel—inadequate.'

'I'm sure you could never be that.' His voice sounded hard. 'I don't think Carlo is going to live and she needs a woman's understanding. Are you still there, Harriet?'

'Yes, I'm here,' she said. 'I'll come in the morning and do what I can for Emmy.'

But mostly for you, she thought.

'Thank you, Harriet.' There was a lengthy pause. 'Somehow, I'll make it up to you. If Carlo pulls through it will be a miracle.'

'Does he recognise Emmy?'

'Oh, yes, he knows she is there. He is not unconscious—just weak. I don't understand what he has done to himself. He is like a skeleton and catching pneumonia hasn't helped. I will stay here, of course, to look after Emmy,' he added. 'Will you tell my grandmother?'

'Yes.'

'Harriet—thank you,' he said again. 'This means a lot to me. I'll pick you up at the apartment.'

She put down the receiver, standing quite still for a moment before she rejoined the Contessa who had come to the *sala* door.

'There is no encouraging news,' she said. 'Tarquin asked me to tell you. He wants me to go to Rome in the morning.'

'And what have you promised?' Renata asked, watching her closely.

'I said I would go. Emmy needs someone to talk to.'

'I see.' The Contessa moved towards the staircase, leaning on her ebony stick. 'Will Tarquin come for you?' she asked.

'He is sending a car. He won't want to leave the hospital when Carlo is so ill.'

'Is he unconscious?'

'Not completely. Tarquin said he had recognised Emmy.'

'That may help.' They mounted the first few steps. 'We can only hope that he lives,' said Renata.

In the morning Harriet was up and waiting on the terrace when the hired car came swiftly along the drive between the orchard trees. The dew was still on the grass and the sun had not yet risen above the distant hills, but there was a golden light in the sky which seemed like a promise.

The sound of bells followed them all the way to Rome, ringing out from hidden chapels or crashing from lofty campaniles as they passed through the little hill towns on their way. It was Sunday and the bells were the only sound on the early morning air as the people converged on the churches, hurrying to prayer. The sun came up, gilding the whole landscape with light as it spread its glorious warmth on the waiting earth.

The journey back seemed twice as long as it had been on the way down, although there was far more to think about now. Tarquin had found Carlo and Emmy was by her husband's side. Would it make a difference, stirring him to fight for his life?

Graziana was still in bed when she put her key in the front door of the apartment.

'Hi!' she said sleepily, coming to her bedroom door. 'I didn't think you would get here so soon.'

'You knew I was coming?'

'Tarquin phoned. He said Emmy needed you, though I can't see why since he's doing everything he can for her.' Graziana made her way to the kitchen, clutching her dressing-gown about her like a toga. 'I'll put the kettle on,' she offered.

'Not for me,' said Harriet. 'Tarquin may be here at any moment.'

'I need some breakfast,' Graziana pointed out. 'I went to a party last night and we were late home.' She came back into the living-room. 'How bad is it?' she asked.

'He's very ill. I don't think Tarquin would have sent for me otherwise.'

'To be with Emmy,' Graziana reflected. 'Do you think it was his idea?'

'It was Emmy's. Somehow I feel sure of that.' Harriet sat down in the nearest chair without removing her coat. 'At first I felt that I couldn't like her, Graz, but then I just couldn't help feeling sorry for her. She'd made a lot of mistakes, but haven't we all? And now I think she's genuinely sorry for all the trouble she caused during these first years of her marriage.'

'It was plenty,' Graziana returned dryly. 'She just managed to bankrupt her husband and put him literally on the streets. Tarquin has told me about your meeting on the Steps and the two portraits, and I think Emmy deserves all she's got.'

'I suppose she does, in one way,' Harriet allowed, 'but we can't tell her that. It's a bit like kicking a man when he's down, and Tarquin does believe she's trying.'

'She tried hard enough in his direction once before,' Graziana said. 'She would cheerfully have added his scalp to her belt if he hadn't been too strong a character to allow it. Instead she settled for Angelo.' Her tone became bitter. 'And he, like a fool, decided to play her little game.'

'I think that's all over now.' Harriet sat back in the chair. 'I can't answer for Tarquin, but I think Angelo has taken notice of the red light. He's not half so mettlesome as he used to be. I think he wants to settle down.'

'So he says.' Graziana ground the coffee beans with more energy than was strictly necessary. 'He's asked me to marry him.'

'Graz! When did all this happen?' Harriet exclaimed.

'Nothing has "happened". Not yet.' Graziana turned

almost carelessly from the percolator. 'I think he should be given time to change his mind.'

'Do you mean you're keeping him dangling to teach him a lesson?'

'You could say that.'

'For how long?' It was difficult for Harriet to resist a smile.

'Not too long, but I think he deserves to wait. Don't you?'

'You know him better than I do.'

'I'm not too sure about that,' Graziana reflected. 'He told me in the early hours of this morning that you'd given him a severe talking to and knocked some sense into his head.'

'I'm glad what I *did* say finally got through to him.' Harriet crossed to the window to look out. 'Do you think something might have happened?' she asked uneasily. 'I thought Tarquin would have been here by now.'

Graziana poured the percolated coffee into two stone mugs.

'You know hospitals,' she said. 'They keep you waiting. Drink your coffee and relax. Tarquin will come as soon as he can.'

Harriet accepted the mug of steaming coffee but refused the biscuit Graziana offered.

'It's going to be a terribly long day,' she reflected.

It was two o'clock before the door bell rang.

'You may as well answer it,' said Graziana, clearing away the remains of their frugal lunch. 'It just has to be Tarquin.'

There had been no phone call, no note—nothing. Harriet went towards the door with a heavy heart.

When she opened it Tarquin was standing outside with some flowers in his hand.

'What happened?' she asked automatically.

'There was some sort of crisis. We had to stay there.' He passed her on the way to the inner room. 'I couldn't leave Emmy to face it alone.'

'Carlo——?'

He shook his head.

'He came out of it, whatever it was, but I think it must

have been tough going. I've left Emmy at the hospital,' he added. 'She seems to be made of steel.'

'It sometimes happens.' Graziana came to take the flowers. 'You'll have something to eat?' she asked.

'Some coffee,' he agreed.

He drank it standing in front of the window, looking out across the rooftops to the trees in the Borghese gardens.

'What happens now?' Graziana asked. 'Are you going back to the hospital?'

He hesitated.

'They said to leave it for a while. They've given Emmy a room to sleep in for an hour or two. I thought myself superfluous, so I came away.' He looked drawn and tired. 'I'll go back, of course, later on.'

Harriet went to her room to unpack her suitcase, looking at her reflection in the mirror on her dressing-chest with no very clear train of thought in her mind. She saw a tall, pale girl with red hair and haunted eyes, a smudged replica of herself as she had been two months ago when she had first returned to Rome. Was this what loving without hope could do to you? she wondered. Was this what it would be like for the rest of her life?

Turning from the mirror, she squared her shoulders. Not for me, she thought. I've got to fight my way back to normal. I've got to make some sort of life for myself in the future out of all this. When Angelo and Graziana marry—because I think they will—I must go back to London and Graziana can help in the shop.

'I may have got the wrong facts,' Graziana was saying when she reappeared in the living-room doorway, 'but you'll have to sort that out for yourself. Meanwhile, if I can do anything for Emmy you have only to ask.'

Tarquin nodded, pacing back to the window like a caged animal whose only desire was to be free.

'Perhaps we could walk for a while,' he suggested, 'before we go on to the hospital.'

Harriet put on her jacket, taking up her shoulder bag to accompany him downstairs.

They walked in the Borghese gardens under the ilex

trees with the sweet scent of magnolias in their nostrils and the sun warm on their backs. It was Sunday and every family in Rome seemed to have gathered round the lake or on the wide terraces of the Piazzale del Pincio, but there was comparative seclusion to be found among the pine-bordered paths of Siena where the shadows were deepest.

They walked without speaking for a time and gradually it seemed to Harriet that some of the tension had gone from her companion's face. His mouth had relaxed a little and the tiny pulse which she had seen beating at his temple had subsided, although his hands were still thrust deeply into the pockets of his jacket, clenched unconsciously as his fears took wing.

Almost by mutual consent they avoided the subject which dominated both their thoughts. They spoke of Cerano and not of Carlo, as they might have done.

'I have a great responsibility to the estate,' he explained. 'No matter how kind and affectionate my grandmother may seem, she must often think of her own sons and the appalling loss she suffered at the hands of a maniac dictator. But for Mussolini, my uncles would be there now, tending the vineyards and making wine as their forefathers did for generations, good, honest Italian citizens who had no desire to go to war.'

'Tarquin, she's very proud of you,' Harriet objected. 'She sees you as the real salvation of Cerano.'

He smiled.

'But she also sees me as an Englishman,' he said. 'She has not quite come to terms with my tainted blood!'

'I think you could be wrong,' she said as they reached the top of the hill. 'She feels you've brought a sort of leavening into the de Filippo strain.'

'Is that what it is?' His smile deepened. 'Heaven knows, I am willing to try.' He paused. 'I know she worries about Angelo, but perhaps some of your "leavening" may be at work there. He seems to be settling down. How do you find him in the shop? Not too careless, I hope.'

'He was bound to make the odd mistake in the beginning.' They turned to go back down the hill. 'It isn't an easy trade to master and it can't be done quickly. He was restless when he first came back to Rome. Now——'

He looked at her sharply.

'Now I think he may have a goal in view,' Harriet added carefully. 'I think he intends to marry quite soon.'

He increased his pace until she had almost to run in order to keep up with him.

'Are we going to be late?' she asked, glancing at her watch.

'Not necessarily, but we'll take a cab.'

To Harriet's delight he signalled to one of the old horse-drawn carriages lined up at a nearby rank and they bowled off in state behind a high-stepping pony with the driver flourishing his whip to warn the pedestrians in his way.

'They don't take a blind bit of notice!' Tarquin pointed out as they were forced to slow down, 'but I still think this is the best way to travel around Rome.'

The ideal way, Harriet decided, sitting back against the sunwarmed leather of the cushioning while the gentle evening breeze fanned her cheeks. At a pavement stall they stopped to buy roses for Emmy, who was so fond of flowers.

'I know she won't have time for them,' she said, 'but quite often they help.'

Tarquin paid for the flowers without replying. The tenseness had crept into his face again and his eyes were remote.

When they reached the hospital he paid off the carriage, adding a generous tip which prompted the driver to sweep off his stove-pipe hat as he flourished his whip in salute.

'Grazie, signore! Signora!' He swept Harriet a special bow. 'Bella! Bella!' he added with a wicked smile.

Clutching the huge bouquet of pink roses close to her breast, Harriet followed Tarquin up the steps. Signora! The little man had made a great mistake, but for a moment she savoured the sweetness of being mistaken for Tarquin's wife. The Bella! Bella had been the usual extravagance of the Italian temperament, but it left a warm glow in her heart as the doors swung to behind them.

Tarquin spoke to one of the nuns seated at a large reception desk who rang a bell after a swift check through a green filing system, and presently they were walking along a wide, tiled corridor behind a jolly little nursing Sister whose voluminous white robes appeared to engulf her completely. Like all nuns, she had a beautiful smile, but as they drew nearer the waiting-room her face clouded a little.

'You will please to wait here,' she said in halting English. 'I will go to see if the *signora* is awake.'

They stood in the long, bare room for what seemed an eternity. Harriet laid her flowers on the table where newspapers and magazines were spread for their convenience, but she could not bring herself to sit down. Tarquin seemed unable to keep still. He prowled to the window and back again, staring down at the roses as if he couldn't think where they had come from and neither of them spoke because there seemed nothing more to say.

When the door finally opened he swung round to face it, and Harriet looked up to see Emmy standing there in a crushed brown dress with her golden hair in disarray. She paused for a moment, looking from one of them to the other, as if they had come from a different world, before she stumbled towards Tarquin with outstretched arms. The tears were pouring unrestrainedly down her cheeks as he took her in his arms.

'Oh, Tarquin! Tarquin,' she cried, 'he will live! There's hope, and I owe it all to you. No one else would have persevered in the search for Carlo as you have done for the past year. No one could have convinced him to start again but you!' She kissed him on both cheeks. 'I love you,' she said. 'I love you, Tarquin, more than I can say!'

It was an extravagant, almost hysterical gesture which he seemed to understand, and after a little while he put her into the nearest chair.

'You will give him all the care and attention he needs now,' he said confidently.

Emmy raised tear-washed eyes to his.

'I mean to,' she said earnestly. 'I will never let him down again. I'll do anything he says. I'll even go back to Amalfi to live if he wants to paint and we'll work things out together. It isn't too late, even now, to start all over again. I will take him to Amalfi as soon as he is well enough to travel.'

Tarquin put a restraining hand on her arm.

'Perhaps we had better leave all these arrangements for a day or two,' he advised. 'Carlo has pulled through the immediate crisis, Emmy, but he's going to need professional care and a good deal of rest for some time. I suggest that you go back to the Villa Coralo where you can look after him properly. There are too many steps at Amalfi.'

And too many memories, Harriet thought, which only a lot of loving could sweep away.

CHAPTER NINE

IT was a week before Carlo was allowed out of bed and another week before Emmy was permitted to take him to the Villa Coralo.

In all that time Harriet had seen nothing of Tarquin. He had taken her back to the apartment that afternoon, dropping Emmy at her hotel in the Via Vittoria Veneto afterwards, and before the end of the week he had returned to Cerano. Of course, she reasoned, there would be a tremendous backlog of estate work for him to supervise, and the fact that he had never made any secret of his dislike of Rome made it only natural that he should have gone home as quickly as possible.

When Graziana bounded in one afternoon to announce that she was on her way to the Villa Ilena 'on urgent business' her heart seemed to miss a beat.

'Is anything wrong?' she asked, thinking of Tarquin.

'On the contrary,' laughed Graziana, 'I am about to give everyone an enormous surprise.'

'You don't mean——?'

'Yes, I do, Harri! Angelo and I are going to be married.'

Harriet gasped.

'And you haven't said a word! I thought——'

'We decided not to wait, after all.' Graziana's cheeks were flushed, her eyes bright with joy. 'I've got my diploma and that makes it easier to ask.'

'I don't think anyone is going to disapprove,' Harriet assured her. 'Where is the happy fiancé?'

'Isn't he here?' Graziana moved towards the inner room. 'He'll have to stop taking these long *siestas* in the middle of the day. They're absolutely demoralising!'

'He went out an hour ago, saying he had some shopping to do,' Harriet explained.

176

'My ring!' Graziana cried. 'I have pointed it out to him, but how does he know it will fit? Angelo never stops to think,' she declared on her way to the door. 'I must go in search of him.'

'Are you going straight to Cerano when you find him?' Harriet asked with a catch in her throat.

'I guess so.' The younger girl paused with her hand on the doorknob. 'I hope it's not going to be too great an ordeal,' she said. 'I've written to America to my parents, but somehow Grandmother seems to be the one person I have to *ask*. She still feels she's the head of the family and I get a sinking sensation when I remember that Angelo and I are cousins. It's the sort of thing she might bring up if she wanted to put a spoke in our wheel.'

'I don't think she will,' said Harriet. 'After all, she'll be gaining a granddaughter twice over. She's very conscious of family—keeping you all together.'

'We'll have the wedding as soon as possible,' Graziana ran on, 'though there'll be lots to do. My family will come over from Iowa and possibly Aunt Donna and the girls from Texas. Harri, it would be lots of fun if you could be my bridesmaid, though I'd have to ask the two girls as well.'

Harriet swallowed the lump in her throat.

'We'll see,' she said. 'I could be back in London by the time you're married.'

'You wouldn't!' Graziana protested. 'Surely you wouldn't, Harri? I'm going to need you. Grandmother will need you, too, to cope here while she arranges everything at the villa. You know she won't delegate authority when it comes to a family wedding.'

'Better ask her first.' Harriet bent to kiss the flushed cheek. 'Graz, I hope you're going to be very, very happy,' she said.

'And you!' Graziana was eager to include the whole world in her personal joy. 'You've no idea how excited I feel, and I was going to be deadly calm about it all! The veritable Ice Maiden in person. It's amazing how we change!'

'I thought you were going to the villa to ask the Contessa's permission,' Harriet laughed.

'We are,' Graziana agreed. 'I'll take the ring off before we get there, but I just have to find out how it would feel.'

When she had gone Harriet turned back into the shop, which now seemed curiously empty. She had been kept busy all morning and during the early part of the afternoon, but now the flow of customers had dwindled and she was finally alone. She could hear Dino hammering away behind the curtains, enlarging a cupboard in the inner room, but she did not offer to help. When it was almost closing time she took the most valuable items of jewellery from the window to lock them in the safe overnight.

'I'll put these away, Dino,' she said, 'and then I think we may as well lock up.'

He nodded, laying aside his tools to go into the shop. Dino would always be there, Harriet thought, the faithful employee who would never fail the Contessa no matter what happened.

When she opened the safe door she was immediately confronted with the bronze Cupid standing on his marble plinth with his wings spread as if ready for flight and the poised arrow seemed directed straight at her heart.

How foolish, she thought, closing the door sharply on the little god's eager smile. He was never mine!

Before she had crossed the room she was aware of voices in the shop itself and all the blood in her body seemed to rush to her heart as she recognised them—Dino and Tarquin in earnest conversation on the other side of the curtains!

Tarquin drew them back almost immediately.

'I'm sorry to be so late,' he said, 'but I won't keep you a minute. I've come for the Cupid. I would like to give it back to Carlo and Emmy—as a sort of second wedding present.'

She stood looking at him, seeing how brown and fit he was, his dark hair brushed back carelessly from his brow, his image that of the happy and contented countryman. This was the way he wanted it to be; this was how it should be. He was a man of the soil, broad-shouldered and strong, his clear grey eyes looking steadily into the future.

'I'll get the Cupid,' she offered. 'It's in the safe.'

He followed her through to the inner room.

'I'm sorry we're in such a muddle,' she apologised, 'but we took a consignment from Milan this morning and it is still waiting to be priced.'

'For which you need Angelo,' he said sharply. 'Surely he hasn't gone off and left you with all this extra work.'

'No,' she defended his absent brother, 'he wouldn't do that. He's been working very hard these past few days while I cleared up a backlog of correspondence. As a matter of fact,' she added slowly, 'he has just left for Cerano.'

He turned from the safe, his eyebrows raised in surprise.

'With Graziana,' she said deliberately. 'They are going to be married. Eventually, I suppose I should say, because they have gone to ask the Contessa's permission.'

'She is the head of the family,' he said. 'It's traditional, but I didn't think Angelo or Graziana would acknowledge the fact.'

'You've no idea how old-fashioned young people can be in that respect,' Harriet laughed, opening the safe for him.

He was looking at her closely, trying to penetrate the barrier of reserve which she had raised between them.

'How do you feel about it?' he asked bluntly.

'Me? I'm delighted,' Harriet smiled. 'I think it's the best thing that could happen to both of them. Angelo seems to have sown all his wild oats now and is ready to settle down.'

'And Graziana?' he asked, looking in at the little Cupid in his steel tomb.

'She has always been in love with him,' Harriet decided. 'Oh, they squabbled a lot and went into a huff with one another now and then, but it meant nothing. In a good many ways Graz is the right person for your brother. She won't stand any nonsense and she'll tell him outright just how she feels.'

'And you believe that to be a recipe for lasting affection?'

'It saves a lot of trouble and a good deal of misunderstanding,' she said briefly.

He did not answer that, standing aside as she took the lovely bronze statuette out of the safe.

'Shall I parcel it?' she asked, aware of the sudden tension in the atmosphere.

'If you could find a suitable box——'

They were standing facing each other with the little god of love between them and Harriet bit her teeth into her lower lip to steady it as she gave him the statuette to hold.

Their fingers touched as he took it from her, sending a strange, wild fire through her veins, and suddenly it was more than she could do to meet his eyes, but he had taken the Cupid and she was free to go.

'I'll find a box,' she said unsteadily. 'There are dozens of them in the shop——'

When she came back he was studying the Cupid with a contemplative smile.

'How is Carlo?' she asked in a calm, flat voice.

'Putting on weight as rapidly as a Christmas turkey!' he declared. 'Emmy is over-feeding him and the sun is doing the rest.'

'Are they still with you?'

'They are at the Villa Coralo. Emmy likes the estate, but eventually they will return to Amalfi. Carlo would like to go on painting, but it won't make him much money to begin with. Perhaps that's where I might be able to help,' he added. 'A light job on the estate would give him time to recover completely and paint as much as he likes.'

Dino came to help with the parcel, tying it securely with the green tape which carried their signature and the address.

'Are you going straight back to Cerano?' Harriet asked, handing over the box.

'I'm afraid so.' Tarquin hesitated. 'Would you like to come with me?'

She stepped back instinctively.

'No, this is purely family, Tárquin,' she said, adding with an odd twist of pride: 'Besides—besides, I have somewhere else to go.'

'I see.' He paused on his way to the outer door. 'Let me run you back to the apartment, at least,' he suggested.

She could not bear to take him back to the apartment, where they would be alone.

'I—have a few things to clear up.' She had to refuse him because her hands were trembling so much. 'I won't be ready to lock up for at least an hour.'

'Anything I can take for the Contessa?' he asked. 'Apart from your love, of course!'

She hesitated.

'I have some papers for her to sign. I was going to send them.'

'They'll get there much quicker if I take them with me,' he pointed out.

'That's true.' She went to her desk to find the letters, aware that she was giving herself time to return to her normal composure by pretending to search for them. 'Here they are! The top ones are the most important.'

She laid them on the glass showcase, not offering to pass them to him by hand this time, and he put them in his pocket and went away.

The days that followed their brief encounter went by on leaden feet. Of course, she was kept busy; of course, there was all the excitement of Graziana and Angelo becoming engaged to take up her attention, and of course she heard of Tarquin from time to time, but it was always in connection with the estate. He was working almost night and day, Angelo told her, to make up for the time he had lost in these early spring days when Emmy had been his only concern as they searched for her missing husband.

Again and again Harriet wondered if he might still be in love with Emmy, but who could she ask about that? Not Graziana, who was so full of her own happiness and the fact that her marriage to Angelo would take place earlier than they had expected. The news had sped across the

Atlantic, and her mother was on her way to Rome. It was six years since she had seen the Contessa and the old lady was delighted. What better reason for her own daughter's visit than to supervise Graziana's wedding in her old home?

Apparently there had been no question of Graziana being married in America. It was to be a completely Italian affair.

'Down to the family lace and the traditional *confetti*!' Graziana laughed when she told Harriet about it. 'Oh, Harri, I'm so happy I can hardly wait!'

Harriet thought of the gift of sugared almonds, the *confetti* treasured for so long from another wedding, but no doubt Tarquin had forgotten the little incident in the Sorrento hotel long ago. They were still wrapped up in the fine lace handkerchief which the unknown bride had presented to her that bright spring day, but the little posy which had accompanied them had withered long ago.

What a fool she was, remembering when everyone else had forgotten!

Throwing herself into work seemed the best way to forget and she was rewarded by the knowledge of the Contessa's gratitude. They spoke constantly on the telephone, but she would not accept the invitations she received to go back to the Villa Ilena.

'You are all far too busy,' she said on one occasion, 'with all your happy preparations.'

There was a short pause before the Contessa said quite clearly:

'I want you to be here for this wedding, Harriet. I have come to rely on you very much. We will close the shop for a week, and then you can re-open it for Angelo when they return from their honeymoon. It is all arranged,' she said in the slightly autocratic tone she employed when she would not be refused. 'You will come here and help as much as you can.'

Harriet was still sharing the apartment with Graziana, who came and went like a happy butterfly, flitting briefly between Rome and the Villa Ilena and Florence, where she was buying furniture.

'Where are you going to live?' Harriet asked in one of the longer pauses of her busy day.

'Here.' Graziana looked apologetic. 'We thought, if we found you another apartment, this would be just fine for us till Angelo can afford a larger house.'

'Of course,' said Harriet, crossing to look out of the window. 'It's—ideal, isn't it?'

Was this the signal that she must go? Not only from the apartment but away from Rome altogether? Well, she had known that it would all have to come to an end, sooner or later, but this was sooner than she had expected.

'Would you like me to move out immediately?' she asked, forcing a lightness into her voice that she was far from feeling. 'I could find an hotel for a while to let you decorate in here.'

'There's no real hurry,' Graziana assured her. 'I can be at the Villa Coralo for a week or two after Emmy and Carlo go back to Amalfi.'

Harriet turned from the window.

'Then they are going back?'

'Quite soon. Emmy is really serious about the painting bit. She doesn't care how poor they are so long as Carlo is happy.'

'And Tarquin?' Harriet forced herself to ask.

'Oh, he's completely married to the estate! Nothing any-one could say or do would budge him, but when Grand-mother finally comes to Rome he will probably "take a wife", as the saying goes. The term doesn't exactly appeal to me,' Graziana frowned. 'Men don't "take" any more. They have to ask, even in Italy!'

'You're so utterly happy,' said Harriet, 'I don't think you really mind.'

'I do, in principle!' Graziana declared. 'You haven't seen my wedding dress, have you?' she added. 'Let's go and look at it, and then you can help me choose the *confetti*. I rather fancy these little baskets made to look like flowers they do so well in Sulmona. My mother is going mad about this wedding without stopping to count the cost,' she added, 'but she was always crazy about tradition, so I guess I'd better conform.'

Harriet sat on a little gilt chair while the wedding dress was fitted for the last time, thinking how ethereal Graziana looked in the swirling chiffon and lace with the family veil lying ready on an adjacent chair. It was made of the finest lace mounted on a tiny coronet of pearls and was far removed from the faded jeans and kerchief which Graziana habitually wore. She looked a completely different person these days, far removed from the inconsequential art student who had roamed the Via Margutta for inspiration or sketched for long days on end among the ancient ruins of the Palatine or the Foro Romano.

Almost as if she had known about the delicate handkerchief hidden away in Harriet's drawer, she left the final choice of the *confetti* to her friend.

'You choose,' she said when a selection was set out before them. 'I find it all so confusing, and already I have doubts about the other "thank you" gifts. A bronze urn seems a bit funereal to me, even though it's filled with expensive perfume!'

'You have still time to change your mind,' Harriet pointed out. 'Wasn't there a second choice?'

'I thought I didn't need one,' Graziana said pensively. 'I'm so full of enthusiasm at the time I'm quite sure I won't change my mind. No, the urn will have to do. It's absolutely Grecian and very lovely.'

Harriet was gazing down at the array of sugared almonds on the showcase in front of them.

'You'd still go for the Sorrento handkerchiefs,' Graziana suggested.

'No! I think you should have something—more local,' Harriet said hastily, picking up a small basket tied with coral-coloured ribbon. 'Why not this?' she asked. 'It's very pretty. The flowers are artificial, of course, but they would last.'

'You think we should have real flowers?' Graziana frowned. 'So do I. Tarquin hates anything artificial and, after all, he is paying for the *confetti* and the urns.'

It was something Harriet didn't know, and the fact sent her pulses racing in the same old, foolish way. Of course, he hadn't been remembering Sorrento when he had offered to provide his cousin's wedding *confetti*. It was probably just an old family tradition which he had undertaken to continue as a matter of course.

They met, inevitably, at the pre-wedding reception which the Contessa gave at the Villa Ilena, but it was a crowded affair attended by so many distant relatives and in-laws from America that there was very little opportunity for conversation apart from a brief 'hullo'! Tarquin was, after all, host in his own home for the first time since she had known him and he had many duties to perform.

Before she went back to Rome with Angelo, however, he came across the floor to where she was standing alone beside one of the marble pillars in the main *salone*, his hand dug deep into the pocket of his white dinner-jacket, his eyes curiously dark as they challenged hers.

'It seems ridiculous that I should be carrying this around with me all the time, Harriet,' he said, producing the cameo necklace. 'I want you to take it.'

She looked down at the exquisite little cameos interspersed along the fine gold chain.

'Do you wish me to sell it?' she asked harshly.

'That isn't my reason for giving it back to you,' he said.

'Then what is?' She looked up to meet his eyes. 'The Contessa is paying me adequately enough for what I'm doing.'

In the overheated, crowded reception room it seemed as if they were alone, and suddenly she knew that he was angry.

'Give me your hand,' he commanded. 'As I see it, you are merely being obstinate.'

He unclenched her fingers, pouring the fine chain with the cameos into the palm of her hand.

'Wear it tomorrow,' he said. 'It will be greatly admired.'

With that he let her go, turning back to his other guests as they started to leave.

Angelo said goodbye to Graziana and her parents, joining Harriet at the foot of the terrace steps.

'Whew!' he commented, 'that was tough going and no mistake! I'm sure I must have put my foot in it somewhere. I hadn't a clue about this sort of thing or Graz and I would have gone off to Florence to be married in peace!'

'And disappoint everyone, including your grandmother and Graz's parents? They're in their element, Angelo, celebrating the first marriage in the family for years,' Harriet pointed out.

He helped her into his car, pulling up the hood because the wind was cool.

'I guess you're right,' he said in more serious vein. 'You've been right about a lot of things, Harri.'

'Such as?'

'Oh, telling me not to be such a fool when I made a pass at you and letting me see that just being a playboy wasn't going to get me anywhere in the end.'

'I'm glad I helped,' she said lightly, 'and surely Graz had something to do with it, too?'

'Yes,' he sighed. 'You women always win! You set out to do something and you end up by doing it very well.'

'Is that a compliment?'

'It was meant to be.' He gave her a sidelong glance. 'What about you?' he asked.

'I'll be at your wedding tomorrow and then I'll go back to Rome, and when you are capable of managing the shop on your own, I'll return to London. I may even act as your agent there, if you ask me nicely.'

He frowned.

'That won't do at all,' he said. 'We need you here, Harri. Everybody needs you.'

She was glad he could not see her face in the dim light or the fact that there were sudden tears in her eyes at the simple thought of being needed.

'It's good to know,' she said huskily.

When he set her down outside the apartment he kissed her on the cheek.

'*Arrivederci*, Harri!' he said tenderly. 'I could have loved you.'

It was typically Angelo, and she went up the dark stairway to the lonely apartment with a tender smile on her lips.

In the morning she went first to the window to make sure that the sun was shining. It was a glorious day, more than fit for a bride, and when she stepped into her bath she was able to sing. Happiness was contagious and it seemed to be everywhere; in the song of the birds; in the bright sky above her head so translucently blue that it seemed heaven itself was about to fall through; in the sound of bells when she opened the long casement leading to the tiny balcony which overhung the street, and in the laughter of children as they ran along the pavement in the direction of the Gardens to play beside the Water Clock.

The hired car which was to take her to Cerano arrived ahead of time with a cushion of flowers in front of it because the driver had discovered that she was going to a wedding. She had thought it best that Graziana's cousins from America should be her only bridesmaids and was going merely as a guest.

The taxi-driver chatted most of the way to the Villa, breaking into song now and then as befitted the occasion, a dark little Italian extrovert so obviously delighted with romance.

'*Bella! Bella!*' he had declared when he had first looked at her in her sea-green dress with the cameo necklace at her throat, and she had smiled back at him under the wide brim of her Leghorn hat as if his unreserved approval was all she really needed to make her day complete.

It was a day to be remembered, in fact, a wonderful kaleidoscope of colour culminating in the wedding breakfast, which was set out in the loggia of the villa overlooking the terraced gardens and the distant lake.

Graziana, who had been nervous at first, was now so full

of joy and happiness that it had to be infectious.

'I want everyone to feel the same way,' she declared, adjusting the family lace on her dark head once again. 'We ought to have weddings more often, I guess. Look at Emmy and Carlo! They're living their big day all over again. Harri,' she added beneath her breath, 'why don't you marry Tarquin?'

Brides were privileged to say the most outrageous things, but Harriet was saved an answer by this bride's mother who came up to remind her that the *confetti* should now be handed round since it was almost time for them to leave on their honeymoon.

'For heaven's sake!' exclaimed Graziana, 'I'm not going to be allowed to enjoy my own wedding!'

When the trolley with the gifts was wheeled on to the terrace she made her rounds of the wedding guests very prettily, helped by her dark-eyed sister who had arrived from America only the day before. Harriet watched her taking the tiny baskets of almonds, one by one, from the larger, ribbon-decked basket which Angelo carried for her, and suddenly it seemed that she was back in Sorrento with Tarquin by her side and all the world was full of sunshine.

'Make your choice!'

Tarquin had taken the basket from Angelo and was holding it out to her.

'Harri chose them,' said Graziana. 'I wanted her to have some share in my wedding preparations.'

Harriet looked up into Tarquin's eyes, seeing the little flame that burned there as he looked at her.

'They're all the same,' she said.

'Not all of them.' He singled out a coral-coloured basket. 'How about this one?'

She took it from him as he handed the larger basket back to his brother.

'Thank you, Graz,' she said to the smiling bride. 'I'll keep it always.'

Tarquin followed her to the edge of the terrace.

'What did you do with the other almonds?' he asked. 'The ones from Sorrento.'

'I—ate them.' She turned to him defiantly. 'They weren't going to last for ever.'

'You *ate* them!' There was a hint of laughter in his eyes. 'Harriet, you're not going to tell me that you ate health and wealth and love and happiness in marriage at one fell swoop!'

'Why not?' Her fingers fastened over the almonds she held now. 'It's—no more than a tradition, after all.'

'Traditions count,' he said, coming a little nearer, 'especially here in Rome. You see,' he added, drawing her forcibly into the loggia where the shadows were deepest, 'we also believe that one marriage encourages another. Harriet, I've waited long enough,' he said, his voice vibrant with a new passion. 'I've been in love with you since before you went away, but I couldn't tell you that when there was so much to do. I also thought at first that you could be in love with Angelo, although I don't think I really believed that.'

He bent his head to kiss her on the lips, to seek the silent bargain that would exist between them for ever, and Harriet clung to him with shaking hands.

'It so nearly went wrong,' she whispered. 'I almost went away.'

His arms tightened about her until they were like steel.

'That could never have happened,' he said. 'I would have followed you, wherever you went.'

'Are you two planning to get married?' Angelo asked, coming into the loggia.

'Right away,' Tarquin answered. 'Just as soon as we tell Grandmother that weddings are in the air.'

'She won't lift a finger to stop you,' Angelo predicted. 'Look at her out there on the terrace. She's having the time of her life!'

Leaning on her ebony cane now because she had managed to do without it for most of the religious ceremony in the little family chapel at the far end of the vineyard and during the reception, Renata de Filippo came slowly from the terrace towards them.

'Am I to prepare for another bride?' she asked. 'I told Tarquin he was going to lose you, Harriet, if he didn't ask right away.'

'And I took your advice,' Tarquin said, 'even though it was completely unnecessary. You see, I *was* going to ask right away.'

'And the answer is "Yes",' said the Contessa. 'I am very happy for you, my children,' she added, including Angelo and Graziana in her radiant smile. 'And now you must go and change and we will speed you on your way with all our love.'

Tarquin drew Harriet back into the shadows.

'Don't go,' he said. 'We can wait for them here.'

They waited in the perfumed garden with the scent of flowers heavy on the air and the sun bright in the sky beyond the ilex trees, and all the happiness in the world seemed to converge in that one place. When he kissed her again Tarquin said gently:

'This is your home now, Harriet. Never think of going away again.'

Choose from this great selection of early Harlequins—books that let you escape to the wonderful world of romance!*

*Some of these book were originally published under different titles.